Raising My Titanic

For Papa, with equal portions of love and respect

and thanks to:

Michael and Deborah Viner, the godparents of this book;
Elizabeth, its beloved inspiration;
Bob, its real-life happy ending;
Rebecca, its precious postscript;
and to the memory of Scott Donnelly.

Raising My Titanic

December 23

Well, joy to the world. It's two days before Christmas. And here I am.

There is nothing as depressing as Christmas in Los Angeles. Spent a totally demoralizing afternoon shopping in Beverly Hills. Contended with no parking, crazed crowds, endless gift choices, and no inspiration. Plus, every single woman I passed was better dressed than I was.

To cheer myself up, went into a boutique that was having a sale. Thought no more of giving unto others—only of giving unto myself. Tried on seventeen silk dresses. Total disasters. Finally threw my old dress back on, and left. As I was walking back to the car, I noticed I was getting a lot of interested stares. This was comforting—maybe I wasn't looking so bad after all. A few blocks later, glanced into a mirrored shop window, and realized I had put my dress on inside out.

Slunk home.

Eight o'clock now. Am sitting at my desk, a vision in old sweat-pants. Had hoped to tidy up some, but see this is impossible. The desk runneth over. On either side of me are lists and lists of presents that I don't have time or money or credit to buy; cards that were supposed to have gone out three weeks ago, bills, urgent memos, and in the place of honor by the phone, an empty box of Godiva chocolates. Why do I keep it? I wonder. Do I hope for spontaneous regeneration?

Fathoms deep in the mess are the papers. All evening I've tried to avoid them, but no matter how buried I think they are, they keep surfacing.

All I have to do is sign—and the divorce is final. All I have to do is sign.

Reasons for Signing

1. I will be free to date wonderful guys, all of whom will be nicer than Mitch.

2. I can go out and get the expensive "new divorcee" haircut.

3. I will never have to set foot on another golf course.

4. I can get rid of the damned parakeet.

5. I can take an Adult Education Course at Santa

Raising My Titanic

Monica College without Mitch saying that it's the last refuge of a bored housewife.

6. Maybe I'll have a sex life again. (This should actually be number one.)

7. I can go buy the most incredible swimsuit in creation, and have a Club Med vacation.

8. I can dye my hair any color I want.

I take a break from all this euphoria. I go and look in the mirror. Now, what exactly do we have?

We have before us a thirty-year-old woman. She looks her age. Hair is a nonthreatening brown, discreetly touched with gray. (See number eight on list.) Irish eyes are smiling—could use a little make-up. All in all, I'd give the face a 5 out of a possible 10. Figure does better. An 8. Yes. The sexy bathing suit is a definite possibility.

A closer look. Who am I kidding? I look old and lined and washed-out and no man will ever find me attractive again. Even Molly told me yesterday she wished I looked more like her lunch monitor.

Oh, well, hell. So what if I never do have another date as long as I live? That's still no reason not to sign. If all else fails, remember getting rid of the parakeet.

·　　·　　·

Really. It's no big deal. Half my friends are divorced. They're all doing great. They love their Adult Education classes at Santa Monica College. I'll be fine. And Molly will be fine.

I know that. I know all that. But it all still seems so unnatural. I mean, I got married. I was so sure I would always stay married. Being divorced makes no sense—it's as if the bobsled suddenly fell off the Matterhorn at Disneyland. Or as if a beloved movie unexpectedly changed its script, and suddenly Cary Grant doesn't end up with Katharine Hepburn, or little Margaret O'Brien is no longer able to find the Secret Garden.

Later

Just came upon the antique silver fountain pen Mitch bought me in Carmel the winter before we were married. I remember that day. It was so cold, and he put his coat around my shoulders before he would let me step outside. We had lunch in that little Italian restaurant with the murals of fruit on the walls. Then on the way to the car, we passed the antique store and saw the pen in the window. He said "Betty, you need that. No arguments." He marched right in and bought it, without even asking the price.

I know it must have been a fortune.

Just threw the pen in the wastebasket.

Raising My Titanic

.   .   .

I always loved the way he said my name.

Who am I kidding? This is utterly ridiculous. I can't sign those papers. There's no way I can sign them. Of course there's hope. I'm sure we can get back together—I'm sure there's a way we can work everything out. I should call him up and plead.

I'm going to call right now.

I called. He wasn't in.

I signed. I signed the papers.

December 25

Well, the world's most hideous day is finally over. I wish I were Jewish—that way I'd never have to celebrate this horrible holiday again.

It's all my mother's fault. When I was a little girl, she made Christmas the most wonderful occasion imaginable—a two-week-long riot of happiness. The carol-singing, the tree-selecting, the fudge-making, the present-delivering. Then there was Christmas Eve dinner of roast duck and plum pudding, and Christmas morning with my giant stocking. Even when I was eighteen and in college, Mama still used to fill that stocking. And then she died, and she took Christmas with her.

A pretty nasty thing to do, if you ask me.

And I try to be just like her. This year, I tried so hard to give Molly the most fantastic Christmas ever—and completely failed.

For one thing, I went to hell and gone on my budget, and I bought her every single toy she asked for. Exactly what newly divorced and guilt-ridden mothers are warned by the child psychologists not to do.

And what made it worse was that Mitch ended up beating me to the punch anyway. Not only did he buy her the exact same toys, but he gave them to her early, on Christmas Eve. Even Baby Up-Chuck. That really stung.

(How on Earth did he manage to do it? Give his secretary the week off, and have her scour the town for presents for Molly? The sneaky heel.)

Christmas lunch was another disaster. I found Mama's recipe for roast duck, and prepared it for Molly as a great treat. Not only wouldn't she try it, but all through the meal, she kept asking me politely if I was enjoying eating Jemima Puddle-duck. After lunch was over, I shut myself away in the bathroom and cried like a maniac. Found myself remembering my very first Christmas with Mitch. How we dragged that tree up those three flights of stairs. How he gave me the Anne Klein watch as a surprise. And the little plum pudding we got at the Rose Tree Cottage.

And then there was our first Christmas with Molly, when I dressed her up in a little felt angel suit.

Raising My Titanic

And I remembered last Christmas.

I think that Mitch and I both knew it was going to be our final Christmas together. His gift to me was this computer—but I found out later he'd paid for it out of my savings account. This is not the sign of a healthy marriage.

What a miserable Christmas that was. The token gifts, the fake thanks, the cheerless cheer. And what was really strange about it was that I videotaped the whole stinking day. What on Earth was I thinking of? Maybe I believed that I would one day forget how angry and tense everything really was, and that, if we all smiled on camera, anyone who watched the tape would be fooled into thinking that we were really a happy family. And then Mary Lennox would find the Secret Garden after all.

Hunted up the videotape this afternoon, intending to throw it away. Instead, watched it to the bitter end. More crying like a maniac.

Later

I can't believe it. Mitch came over this evening when I was out with Molly at McDonald's. (Another thing newly divorced and guilt-feeling mothers should beware of overdoing.) He left flowers on my doorstep. Do you know how many times, during our eight years of marriage, that Mitch brought me flowers? Never. Never once. And now, all of a sudden, flowers and a sentimental note. I wish him a truly horrible death.

Spent half an hour in the bathroom, beating up the bathtub with a feather pillow. I once read that this was a sure way of alleviating tension. What it is is a sure way of breaking a feather pillow. Tension remained unabated.

Finally went into Molly's bedroom to see if any relief could be found in there. It could. It always can.

When I came in, she was sitting up in bed playing with the new little ponies that my Aunt Becky sent her for Christmas. (Somehow these ponies had escaped being bought by Mitch and myself.) She looked so wonderful sitting there in her Lanz nightgown, my curly-haired little girl with the stained-glass-window-blue eyes.

I asked if I could play, too, and she agreed—providing I accept the parts of the Wicked Queen, the Executioner, and the Evil Pony who gets his liver torn out and thrown to the vultures. I accepted these roles. The way I've been feeling about myself lately, they seemed no less than typecasting.

We had a great time. My Wicked Queen voice was especially a hit—I really got into that part. It made Molly laugh so hard she begged me to stop before she burst.

I loved that. I absolutely loved that. Everything's okay, as long as I can still make Molly laugh.

Raising My Titanic

New Year's Eve

Tonight, I got Molly all dressed up in her little purple velvet dress and crocheted gloves. Spent nearly half an hour on the hair. Mitch will never be able to drag me into child custody court claiming that Molly's hair was unbrushed.

When Mitch came to pick her up, I was still in my bathrobe. Watched the two of them sail off together, and went back inside. When I looked in the mirror, I saw I had turned into Stella Dallas.

It's eight o'clock now. Molly's bedtime. Avoid going into the bedroom where she isn't waiting for me to kiss her goodnight.

FIVE REASONS FOR BEING GLAD MOLLY IS GONE TONIGHT

1. If I had a romantic date, I would be free to enjoy it.

2. I have a night off from watching the *"Doctor Doolittle"* video.

3. I can take a bath for as long as I want. Stay in the water until I look like a creature from a sci-fi movie.

4. I get a night off from the "I Don't Want to Go to

Bed" opera. I wonder if Mitch has put her to bed. Or if he's going to let her stay up until midnight, teaching her to tango and letting her drink champagne out of her Mary Janes.

5. If I had a romantic date, we could make abandoned love on the kitchen counter.

Checked her room. It smells different without her. On the floor was one of the little ponies. Thought immediately of that Eugene Field poem, "Little Boy Blue," about the toys that wait for their little master even though he's been dead for thirty years.

Left room in big hurry.

This night is very long. I made myself a chicken potpie, which I forgot to poke holes into before baking. First it exploded, then it burned. I ate it anyway. The apartment is very empty. I have made a terrible discovery, which leads me to think I am going crazy. I miss the parakeet.

I feel better when I'm writing. It has taken my mind temporarily off the fact that it is New Year's Eve, and the whole rest of next year, not to mention the whole rest of my life, is a complete blank. I have tried gamely to drum up a few New Year's resolutions, but all that really comes to mind is:

1. Remember to buy Molly more underpants.

2. Throw away dead plants.

Raising My Titanic

.   .   .

Not exactly the stuff to build a new life upon. Excuse me while I go to the refrigerator. I bought myself a little individual bottle of champagne at the liquor store today. A terribly Stella Dallas touch.

Am drinking the champagne. The night is looking better.

I mean, what am I so afraid of? I've lived thirty years. I'm no naive patsy. I've weathered plenty of terrible experiences, and I've made it through many a New Year's Eve. Nothing could be worse than the one where Mitch and I were stranded up in Toronto, and the guy with the gun took my coat.

Who am I kidding?

This one is worse.

Thinking back on all the New Year's Eves of my life, I guess the best one was when I was seventeen. That was the night that Mama and Dad took me to my first grown-up party. What a rite of passage that was. Gone forever were the days of sitting at home with the housekeeper, drinking cocoa and trying to stay up until midnight. I was in the big leagues now.

I spent the morning with Mama at the beauty shop, getting my hair cut and curled for the big night ahead. I had always considered beauty shops to be the supreme height of decadence—but that day, they suddenly seemed to be what life was all about. Then Mama took me shopping, and she bought me my first really grown-up dress: sleeveless black velvet. I felt like a Barbie doll in it—the essence of beautiful teenagerdom.

I sat in the drawing room from seven till eight, and at eight o'clock exactly, the doorbell rang. There was Buddy, punctual as always, in his brown suit and mustard-colored tie. I remember the way he smiled at me—as if he couldn't believe that anyone could look so pretty. He just kept shaking his head and saying "Wow."

Buddy Villiers. To this day, I can never think of him without feeling a pang. Even when he was still in my life, I felt that same way—as if I knew that here was something special that had to be treasured. Because it wasn't going to last.

Since I'm in my cups, and feeling sentimental anyway, I think I'll write about Buddy.

I met him when I was fifteen. Mama came home one day, all excited because she'd just heard about a new coed teen drama group that met every Tuesday night in the Valley. I begged her not to make me go, but she insisted. I had gone to an all-girls' school since kindergarten, and she wanted me to start meeting some boys.

I was absolutely terrified at the prospect. Still, admittedly, I was also getting a little tired of playing leads opposite girls with moustaches painted above their lips, and their hair tied back in buns. So I finally agreed.

I met Buddy the first night. He was huddled alone in a corner, looking as anguished as I did. I laughed, and knew I had found a kindred spirit. There was an empty chair next to him; but when I

Raising My Titanic

approached it, he told me I'd better get away—that he was so nervous he would probably throw up at any second. Naturally, I sat down.

The next week, my chair was waiting for me.

Buddy turned out to be the best friend I'd had up till then. In fact, looking back, I wonder if he wasn't possibly the best friend I've ever had.

It's amazing that, shy as I was, I could ever have made such good friends with a boy. But Buddy somehow just didn't seem like a boy to me. He had this funny little face, with glasses, and this cute raspy voice, like a character out of the "Peanuts" comic strip. Plus, there was his name. How scared can you be of a guy named *Buddy?*

We started sitting together every week. During class, we did all our scenes together, and during the break he helped me with my trig homework. My archrival, Judy Loeb, was also competing to be number one in the class, and Buddy, who didn't like Judy either, wanted to help me beat her out. So he'd patiently try to explain the math to me—and when I still didn't understand, he'd simply do my homework himself.

One night, the girl I'd gone to the drama class with got a headache and had to leave early. Buddy offered to take me home. When we got back to the house, Mama was still up. I had told her all about Buddy, and she liked him, sight unseen. When she met

MARY SHELDON

him, she liked him even more. We stayed up for hours that night, playing the Ouija board, and laughing like crazy people. I hadn't realized until that night how funny Buddy was.

After that night, Mama invited Buddy over all the time: to dinner, on outings, and, the following year, to the big New Year's Eve party. She just adored him.

I knew what she was up to—my mother wasn't terribly subtle. Buddy was sweet. Buddy was cute. Buddy was dependable. Buddy was the kind of guy she wanted me to marry.

Well, I wasn't having any of that. Buddy was a wonderful friend, but when it came to husbands, I had slightly different plans. I wanted a brooding, Byronic hero—and little Buddy, with his glasses that never stayed on straight, his ability to trip over any carpet in creation, and his collection of Bullwinkle paraphernalia, didn't exactly spell romance for me.

But that New Year's Eve party—how strange that I would look back on that as one of the most romantic nights of my life.

We went with my parents to the big grown-up party, and we danced (Buddy, of course, was a terrible dancer) and we drank champagne (Buddy, of course, spilled it on his tie) and then we went outside on the terrace and looked at the night, as clear as only a California night can be. I remember how Buddy put his arm around me—how comfortable and comforting it felt.

And I remember feeling, in that moment, that my whole life

Raising My Titanic

was beginning. Looking down at those lights, I knew that tonight was the start of my grown-up life. My real life. The curtain was rising at last. I had my pal, my Buddy, for support, and all the rest would soon be coming. The fantastic years in college; the great, exciting career; and the brooding Byronic hero who would make my life heaven, make my life hell, and marry me.

It was twelve o'clock. I kissed Buddy on the cheek, and waited for my grown-up life to begin.

Well, all the rest, I realize, as I sit here in my terry cloth robe, and my bottle of champagne for one, has been an anticlimax. Life as a grown-up has given me a lot of the things that I wanted, but it just hasn't been the fun I thought it would be.

How really strange—that the best moment of it all should have been with Buddy, standing on that balcony, with his arm around me, waiting for it all to begin.

Since I'm on the subject, I guess I'll tell you the rest of the Buddy story, depressing though it is. The April after the New Year's Eve party, college acceptances came out. Buddy called me up to say that he'd been accepted to both UCLA and Duke. I took him out to Swenson's for a hot fudge sundae to celebrate. I knew that Duke was his first choice, and told him how much I'd miss him when he went away. There was this long pause; and then Buddy said that he wasn't sure he wanted to go, after all. That he didn't want to leave me.

•   •   •

I cannot fathom why, in all that time, I had never guessed that Buddy was in love with me. It just somehow never occurred to me—I guess because I was never in love with him. But knowing it now spoiled everything.

I tried to be tactful. I told him I was flattered, but that I was too young to be thinking of getting involved with anyone; and I encouraged him to go to Duke. I'll never forget the way his face looked when I told him that.

He went off to North Carolina in September. For three years he wrote me letters—letters I think I still have somewhere. And then finally he wrote me one saying he'd met a wonderful girl and was getting married.

By that time I had met Mitch—the ultimate, brooding Byronic hero—and was pretty close to getting married myself. But still, it was funny. Even though we hadn't been in each other's lives for years, I didn't like getting the announcement saying that Buddy had found someone else.

I haven't heard from him since. You'd be amazed at how often I think of him, though. One thing I'm sure of, he's ended up fine. He's probably putting on plays in an experimental little theatre somewhere—that was always his dream—and happily married, with tons of kids who look like tiny "Peanuts" characters.

I admit, I sometimes used to wonder, when Mitch and I started having all the problems, what my life would have been like if I

Raising My Titanic

had been able to fall in love with Buddy, all those years ago. And I know for a fact that it was something Mama never stopped wondering about. Only a few months before she died, we were watching a ballroom scene in a TV movie, and she suddenly started laughing. I asked her what was so funny. "Buddy Villiers," she said. "I'm just thinking about how badly he used to dance."

Well, I'm good and sloshed. Happy New Year.

January 1

Happy New Year. In spite of quite a heroic-sized headache, I did something quite spontaneous. I guess all of last night's nostalgia for my youth got the better of me, and I ended up spending the morning driving Molly around Los Angeles, giving her a tour of the fifteen different houses I grew up in. She couldn't seem to understand why my family had moved so much, and why some of the houses were so grand and beautiful, and others were so dinky. Funny—at the time, it never seemed strange to me. I tried to explain that my father had been an independent film producer, and that some years were good and other years weren't so good. She just looked at me darkly and said, "When *I* grow up and become an independent film producer, *all* my years are going to be good."

It was strange, but every single one of those houses—even the rotten little apartment on Shoreham Drive where we lived during Dad's worst year—seemed like home to me. Much more like home than the place in the Valley where I live now, pretending to be a grown-up.

I really miss being a child. And I miss my parents. I realize how much I'd forgotten—but seeing those homes today brought it all back. The little house on Burton, where Dad would make me pancakes on Sunday (he called it "Funday") morning. The huge house on Mapleton where Mama and I played jacks. (I could beat every kid in the sixth grade—Diana Sherman excepted, of course—but I couldn't beat my mother.) The beach house in Malibu where they caught me smoking in the bathroom.

I miss them so much. When I was five years old, they used to tease me about how much they were going to enjoy spoiling my children someday. I used to tease back and say I wouldn't even let them near my kids. If only they were here now. I'd let them spoil Molly as much as they wanted. Oh, wouldn't it be wonderful if they were here right now, spoiling Molly.

God, I feel depressed.

Well, at least I still have Los Angeles. That at least will never die. And I will never leave it. So many of my friends complain about this city, but I wouldn't live anywhere else. Bring on your smog. Bring on your riots and your floods. Bring on your five o'clock traffic on Coldwater Canyon. This is my city, with all my memories. When that big earthquake comes, you can bet I'll be here for it, buried in the rubble, and rediscovered thousands of years

Raising My Titanic

later—a poignant figure, wearing sweatpants and drinking cappuccino—like in an image from Pompeii.

January 2

Started back to work today. Work has not changed since I left it six days ago. I realized I'd been secretly hoping that, on Christmas Eve, Peter would have been visited by three spirits—and that he would have come in this morning, and given Betty Cratchett a great big raise. But the only person who visited Peter at Christmas was his alcoholic brother, whom he can't stand.

Actually, seeing the old buzzard this morning, I realized that I'd missed him over the holidays. To torture him, I told him so; it had the desired effect. He shuddered horribly. I could feel his pain clear across the room.

One good thing about Peter. With all of his tantrums and his brooding and his dramas, he's such an obvious mosquito in my life that he takes my attention off the subtler issues—like being newly divorced and an unfit mother.

Work was hellishly crazy this morning. Peter threw eleven separate tantrums, a new personal best. I ask myself—why am I working for this man? Why do I put up with this? I totally believe in the cosmic plan, that nothing happens without a reason, but Peter's and my relationship defies all logic.

I first met him five years ago. I was doing freelance editing at the time, and one day this man called me out of the blue. He said he needed some copyright information on one of my father's old movies, and we got to talking.

In a misguided moment of curiosity, I asked him about himself. He said he ran a books-on-tape company called Bookworm. And then, for the next hour and a half, he described all the problems it was going through. The bottom line, he said, was that his company was falling apart because he couldn't get any loyal help. I remember actually feeling sorry for him. Feeling *sorry* for him!

Well, the next thing you know, I found myself promising to come over to his office the following day, to look things over for him, and see if there was anything I could do to straighten out his editing department.

The following day I arrived at the office. The place was seething, Dantesque chaos. Peter looked like an inhabitant of the second circle of Hell, with his little saturnine moustache and inscrutable eyes. He grunted "Hi," gestured me toward a desk, and disappeared back into his office.

I had meant to stay the afternoon. I've ended up staying five years. Peter has still never quite gotten around to firing me. He gets around to firing everyone else—usually in the first week. I have no idea what has caused the oversight in my case.

Raising My Titanic

My job has never actually been defined. Basically I do everything. I edit manuscripts, I do production coordination, I produce the recording sessions, I arrange the timetables. But whatever I do, Peter assures me that I do it badly.

I have no idea why I'm still there. I had never really planned to end up like this—my whole life sacrificed on the altar of Bookworm.

In fact, some of the worst fights Mitch and I ever had were over why I didn't quit.

So why exactly do I stay?

1. It's certainly not the money.

2. It's not the thrill of being around celebrities. That wears off pretty quickly.

3. It's not the joy of being screamed at daily by Peter.

I guess the answer is a combination of these three negatives, which alone aren't much, but which together add up to a massive masochistic thrill experienced by few.

I guess I just belong there, is all.

This morning I had to edit a session. Dusty Hearkness (last year's runner-up for Miss America) was supposed to read some Baudelaire for our "Love Poems" tape. The fact that Dusty has a Tennessee accent thicker than Davy Crockett's didn't seem to worry Peter in the least. We booked the recording studio for nine, and she lurched in at ten-thirty, with a green face and two very suspicious-looking pupils. (You get to notice these things, in this business.) She started reading, and by the seventeenth unusable take, everyone in the booth was on the floor with laughter. Dusty threw down the script, screamed at us that we were completely unprofessional, and stormed out. She swore that nevah, nevah would she deign to record for Bookwohm agay-uhn. We laughed so much the roof shook.

Well, I won't tell Molly. She's got Dusty's picture pinned up on her wall, and compares their chest sizes every night.

Later

My friend Cheryl just called and said her agent had canceled their lunch at Spago, and would I like to go with her instead? I keep telling myself that it's bad for my self-esteem to accept these last-minute invitations from Cheryl, but I always go anyway.

I get such a kick out of being friends with the biggest star on TV. It's very against type, but like I say, I believe in the Cosmic Plan.

I first met Cheryl two years ago. After she won an Emmy for *Duet*, Peter was dying to sign her to record for Bookworm. He finally got a meeting arranged, and then on the crucial day, came down with an attack of gallstones. He phoned me from the operating room of Cedars-Sinai Hospital, begging me to go to lunch in his place, promising great things if I managed to sign Cheryl, and threatening instant firing if I didn't.

Raising My Titanic

.   .   .

Cheryl and I met at Le Dome. I liked her at once. It is hard not to like a woman who seems so totally unaware of her own beauty. And Cheryl says she'll never forget the impression I made, either.

I managed to splash nearly a pint of Dijon salad dressing onto the lap of her silk Chanel skirt. She told me not to worry about it, but I felt awful. I summoned a big jar of talcum powder from the drugstore down the street, and went to work. I knelt at Cheryl's feet and began rubbing powder onto the stain. Half an hour later, the entire restaurant was coated in a dainty dusting of white but the Chanel skirt was saved.

I got back up onto my chair, finally ready for lunch; and Cheryl told me she had to leave for her next appointment. As I watched her walk away, I realized that we hadn't so much as mentioned Bookworm or the contracts I was supposed to induce her to sign.

I returned to the office, ready to be fired.

That afternoon, two packages arrived from Cheryl. One was for Peter—the signed contracts. The other was for me—the Chanel skirt.

She and I have been friends ever since.

I love Cheryl. I love her sense of humor. I love her generosity. I love it that she's not spoiled by being a superstar. And I love the fact that she's so beautiful. It's like getting to spend time with a living Renoir. But the thing I like best about Cheryl is that her life is total chaos. Every time I see her, there's some wonderful new installment. Last time, it was the story about the ex-husband with the Mafia princess. The time before that it was the crazed Italian count who wanted to make love on water skis. Oh, it's juicy. And best of all, when I'm with Cheryl, I feel like the sane sister in comparison. Can't wait for today's lunch.

Later

Today's lunch a bust. Not a single wild story from Cheryl at all. No, today's lunch, the spotlight was all on me. Cheryl lectured me for an hour and a half about how it's time I started going out again, meeting men, getting back into circulation. The thought terrifies.

REASONS FOR NOT WANTING TO GET BACK INTO CIRCULATION

1. It was hard enough finding someone the first time around—and I'm not as pretty as I used to be.

2. With my luck, the condom would break, and the next thing you know, I'd be up on an "AIDS doesn't care about race, gender, or status" billboard, smiling sadly.

3. It took me years to get Mitch used to me. Who else is going to understand my four in the morning

Raising My Titanic

panic attacks, love of big band music, and obsession with Victorian children's books?

4. I don't want Molly to grow up seeing a parade of slimy men oozing in and out of her mother's front door.

5. I'm scared to get involved again. Things didn't work out once—what makes me think they would work now? Marriage is like a sack race—even with the best intentions, you do a lot of falling down.

But, to shut Cheryl up, I told her I would think about it.

January 6

Monstrous afternoon. Got a furious phone call from our client Rodney Strong. He's in Cincinnati, directing a production of *The Goodbye Girl.* Apparently, a sick prankster had called his hotel, saying, "This is Rodney Strong—the real Rodney Strong. There's a man going around the country impersonating me, staying at expensive hotels and then not paying his bills...." Well, of course, Rodney knew right away who the sick prankster was.

Peter cackled like a fiend when I pointed out all the embarrassment that his little joke had caused Rodney. But he just hooted all the louder, and went around whistling for the rest of the day.

MARY SHELDON

·   ·   ·

At two, got a call from the day care center. Molly had an earache and wanted to come home. Knew what Peter would say if I asked for the afternoon off. So made frantic calls to baby-sitters, arranging pickup for Molly. Felt guilty the whole time, knowing that if Mitch and I were still together, this never would have happened. Molly would never have earaches, Molly would never be sick a day in her life.

At three, Peter came into my office, scowling. "I just heard Molly's sick. Why aren't you home looking after her? What sort of irresponsible mother are you?"

Gratefully gathered things together and flew out the door. As I passed Peter's office, I heard a familiar voice on his speaker phone. He had called Molly at day care, and was commiserating with her on what a terrible mother she had.

Got home by three-thirty and took Molly to the doctor.

Infection not too bad. Dr. Rubin gave me some eardrops to put in her ears twice a day.

Then I brought her home—and so beginneth the Battle.

Molly will not take the eardrops. No how, no way. Pleas fail. Bribes fail. Molly hollers. Molly screams. I try psychology. I pretend to put eardrops in Big Doll's ears. Big Doll loves the eardrops. Molly applauds.

I then move on to Molly herself. The screams start afresh. "Not yet! Not yet! Now Ballet Bunny needs eardrops!"

Raising My Titanic

Ballet Bunny is given eardrops. Loves the eardrops. Is in ecstasies over the eardrops.

Again, I move hopefully towards Molly. The screaming redoubles.

"Not yet! Not yet! Now White Lamb needs eardrops!"

Half an hour passes. Every toy animal in Molly's room is given its dose of eardrops. Purposefully, I move toward Molly again.

Then she points to the wallpaper, covered with tiny flowers.

"And now all the flowers need eardrops," she tells me. "Each and every one of them."

I swear, there's a Bad Seed glint in her eye.

That's when I lose it. I grab her by the shoulders. She breaks free. I try to push her on the bed. She slithers away.

I burst into tears. I have reached a standstill. My mothering skills have come to an end. I cannot think of what to do next.

Molly looks at me for a moment. She decides to have pity. She mouths something, but I cannot hear it over my sobs.

"What?" I blubber.

She mouths it again.

"What?" I wail.

She sighs with exasperation. *"Policeman."*

I stare at her blankly. Then insight and gratitude dawn like twin stars.

How could I have forgotten the policeman?

"That's right!" I cry. "If you don't take those eardrops this second, the policeman will come and take away all your toys! In fact, I think I hear him coming up the stairs now!"

Molly smiles, satisfied, and presents her ear to me. The drops are put in without any fuss whatsoever. Then briskly, she sits up.

"*Now* what are we going to play?"

January 16

It's Sunday, and Molly is with Mitch. Have been telling myself that I enjoy, nay, that I *welcome* these days off from mothering. And that, with Molly gone, I can have some rare and precious time for Me.

Had great *Ms.* magazine plans for the day. Planned on taking a long brisk walk, putting an herbal mud mask on my face, treating myself to lunch at that elegant new little restaurant on Beverly, reading some Turgenev, and finishing up on the Klein account. Morning actually spent pulling gray hairs out of my head, and afternoon spent watching old *Brady Bunch* reruns. Dinner was cold cuts, eaten by the romantic light of the open refrigerator.

I think I'm better off in front of this computer. I like to make lists. Lists make me feel in control. I will make lists.

LIST OF THINGS ON MY DESK

1. My coffee mug, filled with mouldy scummy coffee from four days ago.

Raising My Titanic

2. Five little Playschool characters—a ghost who glows in the dark, an artist, a cowboy, an Indian, and a scuba diver. My birthday presents from Molly.

3. A photo of Molly, Scott, and me taken last year at Disneyland.

4. The Limoges desk set Mitch bought me in Santa Barbara. (We take a break from the list as I put the desk set at the back of the closet where I won't have to see it.)

5. Seven pencils (three have no erasers, four have no lead) and four pens (none work).

6. Another coffee mug, contents in a worse state of decomposition than the first.

Not terribly inspiring.
Other Lists.

IF I WERE STRANDED ON A DESERT ISLAND, WHAT TEN BOOKS WOULD I BRING WITH ME?

1. *War and Peace* (no more excuse for not reading it)

2. *Little Women*

3. *Diary of a Mad Housewife*

4. *Anna Karenina* (I used to identify with Kitty, now it's Anna all the way.)

5. *Madame Bovary* (ditto)

6. *The Joy of Sex* (only if I were not alone on the desert island)

7. *The Bible* (no excuse for not reading that one, either)

8. Something by Herman Hesse

9. Medical book on home treatment of tropical diseases

LIST OF FIVE THINGS I'M PROUDEST OF

1. Molly.

2. That I never squealed on Stacey Lipton about the algebra final.

3. Beating out Judy Loeb for editor of the literary magazine.

(Ten minutes have gone by, but we can't seem to go beyond this.)

LIST OF FIVE THINGS I'M LEAST PROUD OF

1. Gaining ten pounds in the last three weeks.

2. My latest haircut.

Raising My Titanic

3. The time I got caught stealing the Barbie wedding dress from the toy store.

4. Screwing up on the editing of the *Dombey and Son* tape.

5. Wetting my pants in the second grade.

6. The present condition of my skin. The teenage years are back with a vengeance.

5. Losing my SAT ticket.

6. Forgetting to pick up Molly after art class on Tuesday.

7. That I didn't call Mama more often.

8. That I screwed up my marriage.

9. That I was so mean to the parakeet.

10. That I ate the entire bag of Mallomars this afternoon.

11. That the apartment looks like a pigsty.

12. That I wasn't kinder to Buddy Villiers.

Well, this is striking me as an exercise in pure masochism. I believe we will stop.

·　　·　　·

Rescued unexpectedly by a phone call from my friend Scott. He asked me to a movie tonight, but I told him I'm feeling too grumpy to go. I was very touched by the offer, though, especially since Scott met this real cute guy last week at the Wombat Club and I know how anxious he's been to spend time with him.

I don't know what I'd do without Scott. Just looking at that picture of him and Molly and me at Disneyland makes me feel less gloomy.

I love the guy. He's warm and wise and funny, and he's utterly drop-dead beautiful. I enjoy being seen with him, as much as I enjoy being seen with Cheryl. I think the proudest day of my life was the time the two of them took me to L'Hermitage for a birthday lunch. I could just feel the other diners looking at me and thinking, "The woman must have something incredible going for her—look at the crowd she hangs around with!"

Scott was diagnosed with HIV two years ago, but we manage not to talk about it too much. Frankly, the possibility of Scott not being around forever just will not compute. And so far he seems to be doing fine. Maybe I'm in denial—I don't know. The important thing is, we manage to spend as much time together as we can.

Must take him and Molly back to Disneyland soon. I need a dose of the Peter Pan ride.

Later

Yet another call. This one was from my lawyer, Deke. He says now that my divorce is final, we have a few business things to go over. We're having lunch next week.

Amazing how much better I feel. Two calls in a row from two handsome men. And it doesn't matter in the least that one of them is gay and the other one is married. I feel decidedly perkier and more attractive. Besides, since I've been writing this tome, two hours have passed, and it's now time to go to bed. When I wake up in the morning, Mitch will be bringing Molly back to me. Maybe life isn't so hopeless after all.

January 18

Well, I finally gave in, and got back in circulation. Cheryl (in dark glasses and a wig, so that no one would recognize her) took me out to dinner at the Hamlet, and afterward to a singles bar in Hollywood.

I had expected to get some sort of kick from the evening. At the very least, I planned to use it as copy for my lunch with Scott tomorrow; but the reality of it was more depressing than I can say. All those people trying so desperately to make a connection. The laughter too loud. The casual little touches too much like chess moves. It was like a convention of salesmen.

MARY SHELDON

And the worst thing was that I couldn't even feel superior. There was a mirror behind the bar, and I could see myself the whole time. I was as dressed up as anyone there, as full of forced smiles, as nakedly needy.

Two men came over to us and talked. One was bald, seedy, and in carpeting. The other was much too young, and decidedly coy about what line of business he was in. I assume the worst. (A would-be actor.)

God, I hated it. Is this dreariness really what being single's all about?

Looking around the bar, I played a little mind game, rating all the men from 1 to 10. There wasn't a fellow there who made it above a 3. The daiquiris, however, were a solid 9, and I had several of them.

We left the bar around midnight. Cheryl's car wouldn't start, the tow truck couldn't come for an hour, and we finally ended up being driven home by one of the men we met in the bar. Not even the 3! This guy drove a van with a large skull and crossbones painted on the side. I had him drop me off discreetly at the corner of my street, but I could see the baby-sitter peeking out the window, watching my approach with great interest. Definitely a spy in the pay of Mitch.

I will never speak to Cheryl again.

January 22

Molly in the bath tonight. So plump, so pink. She could have been a child in a painting by Mary Cassatt. I told her "Bad Mama" stories about the awful things I had done when I was her age, and helped her wash her hair. The moment was so completely safe, the clouds of jolly, comforting steam, our laughter at the squirting soap. Then suddenly, still with the laughter in her voice, she asked me: "Mama, why did you leave Daddy?"

I sat there, watching all the safety disappear.

I went through all the things I could say.

Politically Correct Answer: "Because we grew apart, honey. There's nothing wrong with Daddy, there's nothing wrong with me. We just grew in different directions until there was finally no point in our being together any more."

Paranoid Answer: "Why? Why do you want to know? What has that no-good son of a bitch been planting in your head?"

Masochistic answer: "Because Mama is a total failure at everything she tries, honey, and why should her marriage be any different?"

Of course I stuck with the politically correct answer, and this seemed to satisfy Molly.

"Yes," she said wisely. "Daddy likes root beer and you don't."

MARY SHELDON

·   ·   ·

Thought a lot more about her question later on in the evening while I was taking a bath of my own. (Am sorry to say that my own bodily appearance looked less like a painting by Mary Cassatt and more like *The Scream* by Edvard Munch.)

Why did I leave Mitch?

I read somewhere that in any relationship the potential conflicts are there right from the beginning. Like in a well-plotted play. Wasn't it Chekhov who said that if a revolver is introduced in the first act, you can be sure it will be fired in the third?

Looking back, I guess the revolver in our play was shown the very first year Mitch and I were together.

How strange. I find I'm nervous telling the story even to this diary. For me it has such significance—but I'm afraid it will seem so trivial, ridiculous, once it's out of my head and actually written down. If I ever showed these pages to Molly, for instance, would she even understand? Or would she think that I was crazy for leaving her father?

Anyway. From the beginning.

I met Mitch when I was nineteen years old. I was in my sophomore year at Stanford. I wasn't doing too well in my classes, and my Dad had recently died. I was lonely, bewildered, overwhelmed.

Raising My Titanic

Mitch and I met at a wine-and-cheese party. I overheard him talking to some people I knew, saying disparaging things about Liberals. I was furious, I was outraged...and I was intrigued. I had never in my life heard anyone sound so confident. Fascinated, I found myself creeping closer to the group, and listening.

During the next fifteen minutes, I had the chance to hear Mitch denounce, with equal confidence, impressionist art, Strindberg, line dancing, patchouli, people who buy used cars, Velcro, AT&T, and God.

Of course I was horrified by this Equal Opportunity Hater. But some weird part of my brain had a different reaction—it scented a challenge. Here was this young man, who approved of nobody and nothing. Well, I was bound and determined to get him to approve of me.

And it didn't hurt matters that he looked just like the Byronic hero I'd always dreamed of meeting.

As the party was breaking up, I went up to Mitch.

I said, "Actually, you're wrong. Line dancing can be a lot of fun."

He smiled at me—a really nice smile. And the next day, he called up and took me line dancing. It was fun. I sometimes think that that was the first and last time in my relationship with Mitch that he ever admitted I was right about anything.

I guess you could say that Mitch's and my relationship was the traditional attraction of opposites. I was insecure, Mitch was in complete control. I was indecisive, Mitch instantly knew what move to make. I didn't have a clue what I wanted to do with my life, Mitch was going for an MBA. I was emotional, romantic, and liberal; Mitch was a stoic and a pragmatist.

We started dating. Right from the beginning, he was the leader of the expedition. And I was the pack horse. I didn't really mind—in fact, it was comforting being led, being told what to do. My feminist friends were up in arms, but then their fathers hadn't just died.

Mitch loved me—I know he did—but it was always in spite of something: my fascination for the occult, my radical politics, the Beatrix Potter posters I had on my walls. I was always being criticized and warned and taught. I felt he was a little ashamed of me, and maybe even a little ashamed of himself that he was with me.

I wasn't at all the kind of girl Mitch usually went for. He showed me pictures of the girls he had dated before me. Chic, dark-haired premed types. Girls who followed basketball scores, went on skiing trips, and were up on the latest headlines. When we went on that first date, Mitch told me I was different from anyone he'd ever known. And we all know how fascinating "different" can be. Until it gets to be a liability.

As time went on, the "different" part of me, the part I most valued, turned out to be the part that Mitch most wanted to get rid of. I remember the state of agony he was in, the first night I met his parents. First he made me change my outfit, asking, "Who the hell are you trying to look like, Alice in Wonderland?"

Raising My Titanic

Then he re-combed my hair. And finally he presented me with two papers. On one was a list of subjects it was permissible for me to discuss (things like the current basketball season). On the other was a list of forbidden subjects—things he thought I sounded stupid talking about (just about everything else).

The irony is that his parents were nice. They were pleasant, simple people who seemed in awe, even a little afraid, of Mitch. I wonder if before they met me he had given them a list as well. For we spent the whole evening talking about the current basketball season, with terror in our eyes.

And, you may well ask, why did I, a smart and self-respecting young woman, put up with this situation?

The maternal reason: Every so often, Mitch showed a different side of himself to me—an endearing little-boy vulnerability. I loved those moments of insecurity; they made me hope that the whole show of arrogance was just a front.

The self-help reason: I told myself that difficult relationships were the growth ones. That the adoring look Buddy Villiers used to give me in high school wasn't worth anything, while Mitch's habitual look of damning disbelief at the stupid thing I had just said or done was making me a better person.

The real reason: Maybe I wasn't so smart and self-respecting after all.

Looking back, it makes me so sad. It wasn't really a happy

relationship—not ever. Not even at the beginning, when we were most in love. I think I must have cried every day, that first year.

Anyway, that's what things were like between us. Now for Chekhov's revolver.

Somewhere in the middle of Mitch's junior year, he started to get sick. Really, scarily, sick. He lost all his energy, he was so pale he looked transparent, he couldn't even walk down the hall without getting breathless. My father had died from leukemia and the symptoms were horribly familiar. I begged Mitch to see a doctor and finally he did. The doctor did some preliminary tests, and said that there was a real reason for concern. More tests were scheduled, for the following Monday morning.

The four days that followed were probably the worst of my life—worse even than the days my parents died. I think it was the suspense that made them so particularly terrible. Mitch wouldn't even talk about it.

Monday morning came. Mitch had slept through the night. I hadn't slept at all. I asked to go with him to the doctor's but he said no; I'd only be in the way. So I told him that I would be in my dorm room waiting by the phone and asked him to call me from the doctor's office, with good news or bad, the instant the appointment was finished.

He left and I took up my position by the phone.

An hour went by, two hours. Two and a half. No call. I sat

Raising My Titanic

there praying, trying to say affirmations, watching the second hand on the clock. I couldn't imagine why it was taking so long, couldn't imagine what terrible thing the doctor might have found. Finally I gave up even trying to imagine. I just lay on the sofa and cried.

At twelve-forty-five, the phone rang. It was Mitch. Very cheerfully he told me that everything was fine. The new tests had shown that nothing whatsoever was wrong with his blood cells—he was only suffering from stress. I burst into tears of relief. I said, "That's wonderful—I only wish it hadn't taken him three and a half hours to figure it out!" Oh, no, Mitch said. It had only taken twenty minutes. He had been finished with the doctor by nine-thirty, and had been back in school in time for his ten o'clock class.

He was calling me from his lunch break.

And I think it was at that moment that our marriage—which didn't even exist at that point—started to come to an end.

I'm reading this over, trying to be objective. Given the person Mitch is, doing what he did made perfect sense. He didn't want to be late for his class. It simply wasn't efficient to call me from the doctor's office. It was much more convenient to call from the common room at lunch. Especially when, as they say, good news can always wait. But then I think of myself sitting by that phone, crying as I have never cried before or since, watching the seconds ticking away. And no call.

Well. That's my big Revolver story, the bottom-line reason I left Mitch. You can take it or leave it.

January 24

Cannot believe I'm writing this. Cannot believe what happened.

Today was my lunch date with my lawyer Deke. He had said it was to discuss business matters, so I'd been anxious about it all week. But when he picked me up at work, he didn't even mention my finances, so I figured nothing too terrible could have happened. I was amazed when he said he was taking me to the Palm. I don't often get taken to the Palm. Even Cheryl gibbers at the prices.

We got to the restaurant, ordered our lunches, and Deke still didn't bring up what it was he had wanted to talk about. I began to feel nervous again. He was acting very strange, almost manic. And very intense. There was no small talk. The whole time, he kept asking me questions—how was I doing? How was Molly doing? What were my feelings, being divorced?

And underneath, it was as if something were bursting.

Finally, I said, "Deke, what on Earth is going on?"

And he started to laugh. I thought he had gone nuts. Then he picked up my hands very deliberately and squeezed them. His hands were very warm.

He said, "Betty, I've brought you here under false pretenses. There's no business to discuss. I brought you here to tell you that I'm in love with you. As a matter of fact, I've been in love with you for just about forever."

My first thought was that it was a trick—that Mitch had somehow put him up to this.

Raising My Titanic

No, that wasn't my first thought. My first thought was that I've been a little in love with Deke for just about forever, too.

But I didn't tell him so. I pretended shock. Dignity. I withdrew my hands. I told him icily that I was very flattered, but that this could go absolutely nowhere. That I may have made many mistakes in my life, but one mistake I was not going to make, ever, ever—was to get involved with a married man.

There was a long pause, and then he said, "What if I told you I wasn't going to be married much longer?"

I wasn't prepared for that. I don't remember what idiot answer I gave.

He changed the conversation then. To little anecdotes, impersonal stories about politics and the news. I began to wonder if I'd hallucinated the whole thing. But his final words at the end of the lunch were "I'll call you." And he kissed me slowly on the cheek.

Later

Am still in a state of shock.

Wish I could tell someone, but it's all too crazy. Certainly can't tell Scott. He's such a prude, and to him, a married man is a married man—end of discussion.

(But is a married man a married man even if he's about not to be married anymore . . . ?)

The trick is, not to think. I'll look on it simply as a great boost to my newly divorced ego; a fun incident to write about in this diary. And if Deke doesn't call, no big deal.

After all, I always have my exciting life in the singles bar to fall back on.

January 26

When a man says he'll call you, what exactly does that mean? This afternoon? Next week? Never?

This afternoon and Never are perfectly acceptable options—but I'll never make it until next week.

It's been two whole bloody days.

Every time the phone rings, my adrenaline system goes berserk. I rush to the phone with a speed rarely seen outside the Olympic games. And I've taken to answering with a marvelously seductive new voice. "Hello, there." So far three people have asked me sympathetically if I've seen a doctor about my laryngitis.

My mind has also been afflicted. I'm totally unable to recall who's being recorded today and I can't even begin to remember what script I'm supposed to be editing—but get me on the subject of Deke Jameson, and suddenly I've turned into Betty, the Amazing Computer Brain.

Without even trying I find I can remember every tiny detail about him.

Raising My Titanic

I think this is what you call obsession.

For some reason, today I'm concentrating on the thought of his neck. He has a very athletic-looking neck, shaded a little darker than his face. And his cheeks. I can't stop thinking of his cheeks. His skin is very pale, and his cheeks appear almost magenta.

Do I really mean magenta?

Later

I cannot believe what I have spent the last fifteen minutes doing. I have been going through Molly's crayons, testing all the pinks and reds on a piece of paper, trying to match the exact shade of Deke's cheeks. Yes, magenta is what I mean, sparingly applied. (And, as you can see, the word I used earlier, *obsession*, is also what I mean—only not so sparingly applied.)

But Betty, the Amazing Computer Brain does not stop at the mere physical. Heavens, no—I find I can also suddenly remember every business meeting, every social encounter, and every word of every conversation that Deke and I have ever had in the last six years.

Especially:

> The time we danced together at Larry Meeker's wedding.
>
> The time I brought Molly to Deke's office and he ended up giving her his onyx cuff links.

The time I had the awful cold, and he sent his secretary out to buy me lozenges.

And I also remember my reactions.

The dance: I felt so uncomfortable I could barely breathe.

The cuff links: I threw them in Molly's drawer and never let *her* use them.

The lozenges: I threw them in my drawer and never used them.

A classic case of the lady protesting too much?

And I'm still protesting. Am I crazy? He's unavailable. He's married. What do I know about him, anyway? Other than the fact that he's always been nice—all right, more than nice. But a lot of people are more than nice. And they're not married.

Raising My Titanic

January 28

Two more days have gone by. No call. I note my reactions.

1. Fury at Deke for toying with me.

2. Fury at myself for even caring.

3. Pride in myself for keeping my dignity at lunch the other day.

4. Fury at myself for keeping my dignity at lunch the other day—maybe, if I had just shown a little more encouragement, he would have called by now.

5. Huge disappointment that he hasn't called, followed immediately by...

6. Equally huge relief.

My heart no longer races every time the phone rings. And my sexy new "Hello, there" has completely disappeared.

February 2

He called. My brain recognized his voice and then stopped functioning altogether. I believe we made another lunch date—for

Feb. 6th at 1:30, at the Hamlet. This is what I believe. My date book also believes it. I have checked it ten times to make sure.

February 5

I can't believe how stupidly I am behaving.

February 6

I have decided to cancel the lunch date.

Married men do not leave their wives. Remember *Back Street*. Remember *The Apartment*. I don't want Shirley MacLaine's suicide attempt scene—especially since my script doesn't have Billy Wilder writing it.

Later

Maybe, on second thought, the best thing to do is not cancel the lunch date. Maybe the best thing would be to go, and be disappointed. After all, part of the reason I'm so attracted to Deke (maybe all of the reason) is that I really know so little about him. He's always been a romantic figure, in the background, misted by distance into perfection. I bet if I actually spent time with him—heard him tell an

Raising My Titanic

off-color joke, or bully a waiter—I'd see him in a much more realistic light, and my little obsession would be totally over.

February 7

Well, I lost the bet.

The lunch date was incredible.

All morning long, I prepared myself for it. I invented this deliciously ironic, cool persona for myself. I would be like Molly's Bobo the Clown doll. No matter how Deke rocked me, I would bounce back up, complete with composed, Buddha-like smile.

Well, all that fell totally apart the minute I saw Deke in the foyer of the restaurant. And that old savage jungle drum that I jokingly refer to as "my heart" took over.

How tall he is. The way he smells. Civilized but powerful. His blue suit was impeccable. Hoped briefly that his wife hadn't picked out his tie—then dumped this train of thought as not being particularly constructive.

The waitress led us to a table. It was very conspicuously placed, and I liked that. It made me feel safe and innocent—this was just a lunch between friends. Nothing clandestine going on here, folks.

As we sat down, I realized something—that this is the first time in ten years I've had a nonbusiness lunch alone with a man. Not since the day I met Mitch, in fact.

What a strange feeling it was. And how different being with

Deke is from being with Mitch. The attentive way he unfolds his napkin. The way he shakes his menu, as if he expects the actual food to fall off the printed page. The way he jokes with the waitress. I noticed and enjoyed every separate little thing he did.

And Bobo the Clown just lay there in a collapsed heap of rubber.

But what I liked more than anything was the way Deke talked to me. I'd gotten so used to Mitch, and his sitting silently through meals in a work-induced stupor, that Deke's attentiveness almost unnerved me at first. But I quickly got over that.

He talked about his feelings for me—"ranging from euphoria to euphoria"—and his feelings about leaving his wife. Relief, guilt, anger at himself for having stayed so long.

He told me that he met her when they were kids, both counselors for a summer camp. He never loved her, but he was lonely and she was available. They were careless, she got pregnant, and wouldn't agree to an abortion. So he felt he had to marry her. She lost the baby almost immediately afterward and he made up his mind to leave her. But she went into such a depression that she had to be hospitalized. (I know, I know. It's sad. Don't think that I'm not aware that it's sad.) Deke felt that it would be unfair to leave her then—that he had to wait till she was stronger. Well, she got stronger and left the hospital—and soon after that, her drinking problems started.

I remember very well the one and only time I met her. It was at Larry Meeker's wedding. She got drunk and made a fool of

Raising My Titanic

herself with the best man. I remember feeling embarrassed for her, and so sorry for Deke.

Was it after that that he asked me to dance? Or was it before? I hope it wasn't before. I don't like to think that Deke dancing with me was what made her get drunk. No—I'm almost sure it was after.

Anyway, it doesn't matter. He stuck with the marriage, out of compassion for her. For the last five years, though, they've been living in separate bedrooms, hardly even seeing each other. Deke thought it would be this way forever—until that day, last year, when I told him that Mitch and I were separating. He said he practically turned a cartwheel at the news. But he never let on. He wanted me to make my own choice, for my own reasons. He said the last few months have been agony, wondering if I was going to change my mind. But the day the divorce papers were signed, he decided to take the risk and tell me how he felt.

I asked him how he felt, now that he had told me. He just took my hand. I can still feel the touch of his fingers around mine.

He said, "The pity I've always felt for Darlene is very strong. Stronger than any reason I've ever had to leave. Until now."

The look in his eyes. I cannot tell you.

After lunch, he kissed me very gently on my forehead, my eyelids, my cheeks. It was like a blessing. Then he said he'd call me soon, and left.

February 8

He hasn't called. Screamed at Molly all day long. I hate myself. This whole thing is not good for my character. Should I call it off before it gets any more intense? Of course I should. After all, what do I really know about Deke? Maybe everything he's said is a lie. Maybe he's got another wife stashed away in his attic. Well, I play Jane Eyre for nobody, thank you very much.

On the other hand, with all this excitement going on, I have managed to lose three pounds. Maybe we could have just one more lunch—just enough for me to lose the other two—and then I could call it quits.

February 9

Talked to Scott last night. Had no intention of even mentioning Deke, but ended up telling him everything, of course.

Wish I hadn't.

Scott is not at all pleased with the developments. He says that I should stay away from any relationship right now, that any romance I get into at this point would be a disaster. Says that what I need right now is not to replace one man with another, but to replace all men with Myself. Learn to be comfortable with my own energy.

Scott's obviously been reading yet another self-help book.

Raising My Titanic

·   ·   ·

As an antidote to this Puritanical sternness, I called Cheryl. She was thrilled to hear about Deke. Says it's great, and just what I need. Then she added, "And it will be a perfectly safe relationship; he'll never leave his wife."

All in all, I think I preferred the conversation with Scott.

6:00 A.M.

Woke up at 4:37 to find the apartment shaking around me. Shot out of bed, grabbed Molly, and we huddled under the door jamb with twelve of her stuffed animals until the shaking stopped. It felt like an 8 pointer, maybe even a 9 pointer on the Richter scale. I know in my heart it was a warning. God sent this earthquake as a personal lesson to me—that's how displeased He is with my even *thinking* about fooling around with a married man. Thanks, God. Lesson learned. No more Deke.

Later

Just heard the news. Earthquake only measured 4.7. That's peanuts.

February 14

A fun morning. Molly had a great time finding all fifteen Valentines I had hidden around the apartment for her.

And she had a gift for me, too. A handmade Valentine's card, and all of last year's uneaten Easter candy. Some of the chocolates looked pretty mouldy around the edges, but that, of course, did not prevent me from finishing the lot.

Am having lunch with Deke today.

Later

I can't believe what I've done. I can't believe what we did.

We met at twelve. He told me to pick him up at his office and that we would go to the restaurant together.

We never made it to the restaurant.

It was clear the second I walked into the office that we weren't going to. There was this feeling that just filled the space between us, this incredible feeling.

I called the office and told the receptionist that I had the flu and wouldn't be in for the rest of the day. Then we went to Deke's beach house in Malibu, and spent the afternoon there.

How can I explain or excuse it? One minute we were in the kitchen, trying to get his cappuccino machine to work, laughing,

Raising My Titanic

and the next minute he was crying, and the next minute we were in bed together.

Well maybe I don't want to explain it and maybe I don't want to excuse it.

Never, never did I dream that sex could be so wonderful. Or so full of possibilities! Why, in God's name, didn't anyone tell me? To think that I had to wait until I was thirty to find it out.

Later

Still can't believe this new tack my life has taken. Can't believe that Betty the Prude hopped into bed with a guy after only three dates. Can't believe that Betty the Moral is involved with a married man. Again, it's like a familiar old movie has gone totally haywire. It's Lassie suddenly starting to talk. It's Ingrid Bergman not getting on the plane in *Casablanca*. There *are* marvels in the world—real, totally unexpected, and unbelievable marvels.

I feel just like a teenager. Am listening to radio stations I haven't listened to in years. I'm full of that adolescent sense of power—my life is just beginning, and I can't make any mistakes.

February 16

Mitch had Molly for the weekend, and Deke's wife is still away at the rest-cure in Arizona—so this morning Deke and I took off and drove to Santa Barbara.

The last time I was in Santa Barbara was last January, with Mitch. It was awful—one of our "let's get away together and try to patch things up" attempts.

I think the gods take special pleasure in destroying those weekends. We had pouring rain, a mouse in the hotel room, and we got into the worst fight we'd had in years. But going with Deke today, all those memories were transformed.

That phone booth on State Street. The one I'd used to call Scott and tell him that Mitch and I had decided to separate. I never thought I could see that phone booth again without feeling ill. But today I saw it, and it was just a cheerful little spot, full of nice people having nice conversations.

I couldn't believe it. I couldn't believe the change in Santa Barbara—or the change in me. I fully admit—it certainly isn't fair that I should be this happy. But I'm not questioning it.

And I'll do good things with my happiness. I swear I will. I'll be more patient with Molly, work harder for Peter. I'll be loving and forgiving toward Mitch. I'll even give Cheryl her Hermes scarf back.

Raising My Titanic

February 18

Big news. Deke has asked me to marry him. He wants to fly to Arizona next week, tell his wife, start the divorce proceedings right away, and marry me by August.

I said I needed time to think about it.

Later

I have thought.

REASONS FOR SAYING NO

1. Molly. She's met Deke exactly once, for Pete's sake. I can't foist him on her just like that.

2. I am in a vulnerable state right now, and as any self-respecting psychiatrist would agree, should not be making any radical moves at this time.

3. Ditto for Deke.

4. What would people think?

No, definitely no. Let Deke get his divorce. Then we'll date for a year, maybe two, and talk about marriage then. Maybe.

Later

Deke met me after work, and we went for a walk in Beverly Hills. We passed a lovely antique jewelry store. There was a little ring in the window—a beautiful tiny golden band in the shape of two clasped hands. Deke started to cry. He took my hand and said he wanted to buy that for me as my wedding ring.

I started to cry, too.

I know. I know what I wrote in this diary just this afternoon. That it's ridiculous—impossible—totally crazy to even think about getting remarried so soon. And yet, there's this weird, deep feeling in me that says differently. It says that marrying Deke would be the right move. For him and for Molly and for me.

I told him that, and we both cried some more.

So, folks, it looks like I'm engaged to be married.

Wow.

Deke wanted to buy the ring right away, but I said to wait at least until his divorce is final. I know that ring will still be there waiting for me.

February 20

Feel very happy. The more I see of Deke, the more sure of my decision I become. He is a good man—kind, honorable, very sensitive and perceptive. Now that things are certain between us I

Raising My Titanic

want to tell everyone we're engaged, but of course we have to keep things under cover until he's talked to his wife. I think Molly suspects something though. She keeps asking me why I've gotten so nice all of a sudden.

Couldn't keep it to myself any longer. Finally gave up and told Scott the news. I know he can be trusted to keep it secret. I was afraid of his reaction but he took it very philosophically. All he said was, "Well, I guess we're all trying to scratch out a simple tune without breaking our necks." (When he was fifteen, Scott played Tevya in his high school production of *Fiddler on the Roof,* and he never lets anyone forget it.)

I could tell by this answer that he wasn't exactly thrilled, but that's okay. When he gets to know Deke, he'll change his mind.

Then I called Cheryl. Her reaction was much more satisfactory. She squealed and screamed, and plans to start shopping for her matron of honor dress on Monday.

I can't tell you how real that makes everything.

I look at my left hand and picture that little ring on my finger.

I thought I had left happiness like this far behind me.

Later

Deke stopped over late tonight. A new toy store just opened up, and he found a teddy bear for Molly he couldn't resist buying. She was already asleep when he came, so he put it on her nightstand, then bent over and kissed her on the cheek.

What a wonderful stepfather he's going to be.

Next Day

Molly loved the bear. I told her it was a gift from a special friend, and that she'd be meeting him soon.

Later

Deke's a mind reader. He just called, saying he thought it was time that he and Molly got to know each other. So we've planned a movie date for Saturday.

Saturday Morning

Woke with a headache, but I'm not going to let it spoil the day. Have engineered everything brilliantly.

Deke's due over here at three. I plan on devoting the whole morning to Molly. Take her to the park, play with her ponies, do my Wicked Queen voice as much as she likes. She'll be in a great mood when Deke comes.

Later

Well, the park not a great success. Headache worse, and Molly threw up on the swing.

Plus, she is very suspicious of my hectic mood. Keeps reminding

Raising My Titanic

me that she's not stupid, and asking me what's going on. Finally I told her that a friend of hers (note the brilliant strategy here in appealing to the child's basically possessive nature) was coming to take us to a movie.

Molly understandably curious as to who the friend was—after all, not too many of her friends are able to drive, much less have money for the movies. I said his name was Deke, and told her he was the one who had bought her the new teddy bear. She said the new teddy bear smelled funny. Then I reminded her that this was the man who had once given her the onyx cuff links off his shirt.

But it could just as soon have been the shirt off his back, for all Molly cared. She didn't remember any of it.

Headache worse. I think I'd better put Molly down for her nap.

Later

I just went in to check on Molly. Nap not going well. Found her wide awake, sitting up in bed, holding a beauty contest to see which of her Barbies had the sexiest bosom. Put her back to bed.

Later

Checked on Molly again. Found her standing on her table, writing and rehearsing a television commercial for a gun that will put an end to mothers. Put her back to bed.

Later

Checked on Molly again. Found her stark naked, parading in front of the mirror and belting out "Tits and Ass" from *A Chorus Line*. Gave up.

Later

Went in to start getting Molly ready. Found bubble gum sprinkled liberally throughout her hair. Spent the next fifteen minutes cutting the gum out. Molly's hair now looks like a biker's.

Headache much worse.

Later

Went in to help Molly dress. Pulled her new beautiful purple smocked dress from the closet. It cost a fortune, but Deke's favorite color is purple; and he once mentioned he loves to see little girls in smocked dresses. And Molly, too, when I first showed her the outfit, seemed to love purple and the idea of little girls in smocked dresses.

But when I actually tried to put it on her, there was total mutiny. Molly said the dress was ugly and disgusting, and she flatly refused to wear it. It was her Catwoman T-shirt, or nothing.

I am ashamed to say I broke every law in the Mama League. I spanked her.

The doorbell just rang. Oh, my God. Deke's here.

Later

The day is finally over.

Don't feeling like writing much.

Midnight

Have had two glasses of wine, and feel a little better. Have a little more perspective on the events of the afternoon.

Here's what happened.

Deke arrived at three. Molly and I were there to greet him at the door. He was charming. Knelt in front of her and kissed her hand. She said, "yuck!" snatched her hand away, and fled the room. And the afternoon went on from there.

I have never known my daughter to behave so abominably. She sulked all the way to the theater, stuck her finger in her ears whenever Deke asked her a question, and when we got to the movie, she wouldn't let me sit next to him. Either she sat in the middle, she threatened, or she was moving to a whole different row. She ended up moving to a whole different row.

At dinner, she refused to eat, upset her water glass on purpose, pulled Deke's arm off my shoulders when he tried to hug me, and kicked the back of his car seat all the way home.

I was totally at my wit's end. What the hell was I supposed to do? Scold her in front of Deke, and scar her for life? Scold her in private, and let Deke think I condoned her behavior? Ignore her, and give her the cue that nothing was wrong? Be firm? Be understanding? Make a big deal out of it? Laugh it off? No article in *Parents* magazine had ever prepared me for anything like this.

I ended up doing nothing.

When we got back in the house, I ordered Molly to her room, told her I'd deal with her later, and burst into tears.

Deke was wonderful about it all, very understanding. Said Molly's reaction was totally natural, and that once we had started dating steadily, all this would work itself out.

So I felt better. Until he had gone and I went into Molly's room. Found her with scissors in her hand, and her two-hundred-and-fifty-dollar Laura Ashley patchwork quilt cut to shreds.

I stared at Molly. She stared at me. I was the one who broke down first. Seeing her there, tiny, white-faced, mutinous, terrified, surrounded by destruction, I had a sudden insight into how she must be feeling.

I don't know what *Parents* magazine would have to say about this, but to hell with them. I didn't say a single word about the quilt or the rotten behavior. I just held up one finger. "Do you know what this means?" I asked her. She shook her head. "It means Number One. And I just want you to know that, *no matter what,* no matter what, that is what you'll always be to me."

She burst into tears. I went over and cuddled her, and we played with Aunt Becky's little ponies until bedtime.

And now I'm alone with my third glass of wine.

Raising My Titanic

Later

Deke just called. He leaves for Arizona tomorrow, to talk to his wife about the divorce. "I'll call you on Thursday, with news," was the last thing he said. Well, this is it.

Thursday

Deke hasn't called. Well, not to worry. We'll talk in the morning. I mean, it's not the kind of thing you can lead into casually, "Oh, by the way, Darlene, I'm leaving you."

Monday

No call.

Friday

No call.

March 5

Save the pity. I'm over it. All along, I knew it was too perfect to be true. What I wrote in this diary—those weren't my real thoughts on the subject. Hysterical fantasy. Of course. I knew deep down inside that he wouldn't leave his wife. They never do.

March 10

I was having lunch at the Stage Deli with Molly today, and suddenly somebody came toward us. It was Deke. He was with Darlene. I never would have recognized her. New hair, new figure, new face. Boy, those drying-out places sure do a lot for you.

"Betty!" he said, in this charming, smarmy voice. "How good to see you. And dear little Molly."

Molly put her arms around his neck, and gave him a big hug. "I remember you," she chirped. "You gave me those beautiful cuff links!"

And speaking of jewelry, I happened to glance down at Deke's wife's hand. On her finger was an antique ring. Yeah, you guessed it—a tiny gold band with two hands clasped.

March 11

I dreamed about him last night. Dreamed we were in a big mall, and couldn't get together. Every time I'd get on the up escalator, he'd get on the down one, and we kept passing each other all the dream long.

Woke up depressed. Damn.

Did he ever really love me? Did he ever really plan on leaving his wife for me? Or was he like Molly—threatening to run away from home, and only getting as far as the elevator?

Raising My Titanic

I ask myself, and I ask myself, and my questions are like layers and layers of onion peelings, with nothing underneath. That's what's so scary—knowing that there is no bottom-line truth, no trustworthy point of view. I'm sure that, if someone were to ask Deke for his side of the story, he would have a ready, plausible, and (knowing Deke) very moving explanation for what happened. Maybe he sees himself as a noble renouncer, giving up the woman he loves for the duty he despises. Or—a decidedly unpleasant thought—does he consider himself one lucky stiff, saved in the nick of time from a home-wrecking siren?

Who knows? Who cares?

But for a while there, it really did seem like the happy ending had come at last.

March 12

Scott's birthday. Made the mistake of asking him what he wanted for his present. He said that he had always dreamed of going up in a hot-air balloon.

"What an enchanting idea," I told him. "I'll make you a reservation. I'll buy you the ticket. I'll watch you lift off. I'll take photographs of you flying in the sky."

But no good. The whole point, said Scott, was that he wanted to go up in the balloon with me.

I started to say, "Forget it—maybe next year," but his face

stopped me. I knew he was thinking that maybe there wouldn't be a next year. That probably there wouldn't be a next year. So I said okay. We're doing it on Saturday.

I cannot tell you how much I hate this whole idea. I'm scared of heights. I'm scared of balloons. (My God, hasn't Scott ever heard of the Hindenburg?) I'm scared of wind. I'm scared of air!

Serious moral issue: Knowing that I'm going to die on this balloon trip, should I take Molly with me or make her stay home? I mean, if I'm going to die I certainly want Molly with me. On the other hand, if I'm going to die I certainly don't want Molly with me. Choices, choices.

March 16

Well, it's Cancer of the Month time. I looked in my magnifying mirror this morning as I was putting on my makeup, and I saw a weird black speck/lump/mole on my chin that I've never seen before. Great. Just great.

Later

Can't concentrate on anything. Spent most of the day in the ladies' room at work, sitting squeezed on the bathroom ledge under the fluorescent lights, trying to see if the speck/lump/mole has gotten any bigger. It gets bigger by the hour.

Raising My Titanic

Made an appointment to see Dr. Klein on Friday.

Found out from Peter that I'm going to have to do an overnight edit on *Thursday Fair* (600 pages) but I took the news very calmly. It's amazing how little things stop bothering you when you will probably be dead in a month.

Later

Washed my face in very hot water. Looked more closely at the speck/lump/mole. Attacked it with a pair of tweezers. It turned out to be an ingrown hair. Canceled appointment with Dr. Klein.

I cannot believe Peter expects me to edit a 600-page book in one night. The man is insane, and I am, too, for putting up with it.

March 17

Well, tomorrow's the big balloon adventure. I am not taking Molly. I have decided to die alone. I've put a manila envelope on my desk with her name on it. It contains the keys to my safe deposit box, and three letters. The first is to be opened on her graduation from high school, the second on her wedding day, and the third either on her opening night on Broadway or upon her getting into business school. (Depending on which genes, Mitch's or mine, prove predominant.)

Cried mightily during this exercise.

I hate to die.

March 18

I live! Like Frankenstein's monster, I live. The great balloon adventure is over.

Got up at 4:30 A.M. Scott picked me up in front of the building. He was in riotous spirits and color-coordinated clothes. We drove out toward San Diego. He grew more and more garrulous by the second. I grew more and more silent.

We reached the field. The balloon was there. It was like looking into the face of God. No words were possible. No words even came to mind. Well, actually, a few did. Humongous. Terrifying. Get me the hell out of here.

And then, as I stood looking at the damned thing, something happened in me. The balloon suddenly became a Life Challenge. It became Me against the elements. It became my Destiny. I turned to Scott, the light of the Crusaders in my eyes.

He was looking distinctly green. "Maybe you were right— this could be my birthday present next year," he said casually.

I had the grace not to jeer.

I do believe this is the first time in my life that I've been braver or cooler than Scott. It has increased my love for him a million percent.

Came home to Molly, and outlined for her the story of the day—my raw courage and willingness to defy death. She shrugged.

"Ballooning's not such a big deal," she informed me. "Daddy took me over Christmas. I guess I forgot to tell you."

Raising My Titanic

March 19

My mother's birthday. She would have been sixty-five years old today.

Molly and I had a little celebration tonight in her honor. I bought carrot cupcakes and apple cider, and I spent the whole evening telling stories about her.

Molly's favorite was the one about the trip we took to New York, the summer I was fifteen. It was humid, about three hundred degrees outside. Mama insisted on wearing her best silk dress and high-heeled shoes. I warned her that the high heels were a terrible idea, but she wouldn't listen to me. She had to look chic. We walked all over Manhattan and by the end of the day her feet were in rags. I said, I told you so; let's just give up and take a taxi back to the hotel. But again, Mama wouldn't listen to me. Without missing a beat she nonchalantly took off her shoes and continued to stroll along Fifth Avenue. Elegant silk dress and barefoot on the streets of New York, smiling at everyone she passed.

Molly asked me if I had taken my shoes off to keep Mama company. I said no, and she told me I was a bad daughter.

"I would have taken *my* shoes off to keep Grandma company," she informed me.

"Would you have taken off your shoes to keep *me* company?" I asked her hopefully.

"Of course not," she said.

7 1

After I put Molly to bed I continued the birthday celebration my-self, reading over Mama's letters to me at Stanford, looking at all the photographs. God, I miss her.

All my life, she was the compass. And now that she's gone, everything's haywire. I wonder what she'd have to say to me now, what advice she'd give.

Every so often, I try to get in touch with her. Not in any weird Ouija board way, but just by closing my eyes and imagining that she were in front of me again. I ask her for answers, but all I can come up with is the sound of her big, happy laugh.

I miss that big laugh. I miss her little pointy nails tapping on the door. I miss the way she could make everything, *everything* into an adventure. I miss the look of worship that always came into her eyes whenever she was with Molly.

It never occurred to me that Molly would grow up without Mama. In fact, Mama was one of the reasons I wanted to have a child in the first place—I knew I'd be a blithering idiot as a mother, but it wouldn't matter. Molly would always have her grandmother to fall back on.

How could you die, Mama, and leave us alone like this?

Raising My Titanic

March 21

Well, today, to the tune of several hundreds of dollars, Cheryl talked me into having a fashion makeover. How totally Californian. How totally recently divorced. How totally an attempt to recover from an unhappy affair with a married man. How totally a waste of several hundreds of dollars.

I met with this consultant, who upon glancing at my complexion and hair color, announced that I was an "Antique Winter." I rather resented the word "antique." She then proceeded to put together little swatches and snippets and make me a chart as to what colors and fabrics and styles I should and shouldn't wear. No wonder my life has been such a rocky one—I've been spending all my time in the wrong clothes. But all this is going to change now. From this moment forth, I'm going to go around in burnished gold lamé sheaths, jade-green silk culottes, and sapphire-blue rayon jackets. No more pale-pink and cream skirts and blouses for Miss Antique Winter.

After the several hundreds of dollars changed hands, I figured I might as well throw some good money after bad, so I went on to Nordstroms to do a little shopping. Looked at all the gold, jade-green, and sapphire-blue clothes they had. Finally found the perfect outfit and snapped it up. It was, of course, a pale-pink and cream skirt and blouse.

March 22

Well, today has to go down as one of the darkest days of my professional life.

I spent much of the weekend editing down *Thursday Fair* for audio. I actually ended up having to do the damn thing twice—my first script turned out to be twenty-three minutes too long. Finally finished at three o'clock this morning.

Stumbled into work, only to find a hysterical memo from Peter on my desk. Dale Drew, our regular producer, was home sick, and I was to drop all my other work, report to the studio in an hour, and produce the tape myself.

My memo back to Peter was even more hysterical than his to me. I explained that I had seven meetings today, an edit to finish, and three contracts to nurse along. There was absolutely no way I could produce the tape.

And then he said the magic words that changed everything. He said that the person who would be recording *Thursday Fair* was Kingsley Dalton. The Kingsley Dalton. The Kingsley Dalton that I have been madly in love with ever since I saw him in *Hector and Alice* when I was fifteen.

I said I would be at the studio in an hour.

Luckily, I was wearing my lovely new pale-pink and cream skirt and blouse. I spent half an hour redoing my hair and putting on makeup, then (as an afterthought) grabbed the script and headed toward the studio.

Raising My Titanic

He was already there. Taller than I had imagined, his hair a little deeper-colored. Impeccably mannered. Absolutely charming. Even his small talk was fascinating. And better looking than is humanly possible. I mean, we're talking possible android workings here.

I knew from last month's *Enquirer* that he'd recently broken up with his "actress/model" girlfriend. So there was a romantic vacuum in Kingsley Dalton's life. And we all know how nature abhors a vacuum. As we settled down to begin the session, all sorts of wonderful possibilities came bubbling into my mind. . . .

I had no doubt that the session would go beautifully. I would be competent and crisp in my directing, bringing out all of Kingsley's more subtle performance skills. At the end, he would thank me ardently.

"I've never had a better experience at a recording session. You're marvelous. You should be winning Grammys."

And I would modestly bat the complimentary ball back to him.

"No, Kingsley, it's all you. You're so quick to take direction, so intuitive about what I want." And then I would look at my watch and show amazement. "Why, it's only (fill in the blank). I can't believe we finished this session so quickly. Usually, actors take twice as long as you did. I feel like celebrating! Are you free to go have a drink somewhere?"

Yes, he would be free, and he'd love to join me. And then we would spend an enchanted hour together in the bar of the Beverly Wilshire Hotel, followed by several enchanted decades of the most wonderful marriage ever seen on Earth. (And Molly would love him.)

The taping began, and my dreams were right on schedule. Kingsley was wonderful. He *did* take my direction beautifully. And we *were* working amazingly fast. With any luck, we should be at the Beverly Wilshire Hotel in an hour.

And then, when the taping was three-quarters finished, it hit me. It hit me like a poleax to the solar plexus.

I had given him the wrong script.

When I left the office that morning, I had grabbed the wrong, bloody goddamned script. I had taken the one that was twenty-three minutes too long.

I didn't have the guts to go into the recording booth. I simply put on the mike and told Kingsley the news from the control room—that I was going to have to go back to the office, get the right script, and that he was going to have to record it all over from the beginning.

I will say for him that he kept his android good looks. But the charm went away like morning dew.

We finished at ten o'clock this evening.

The final recording's all but unusable—he started developing laryngitis around page four of the retake. And the last words I heard him croak were about how he's planning to charge the company double for overtime, and will never work for Bookworm again.

Came home to a message from Peter saying that he has fired me for good and all.

An Hour Later

I have been rehired. Peter's mother is flying in from Buffalo tomorrow, and he needs me to pick her up at the airport.

March 24

Molly woke up this morning, feeling too queasy to go to day care. I had no choice but to take her with me to the airport, and then later, to the office.

I was afraid that after yesterday's disaster this would be the final straw. I sneaked her into my cubicle while Peter was in the washroom, and hid her behind my desk, with a bribe of unlimited stickers if only she would color quietly and not say a word. Felt like a Dutch citizen hiding a Jew from the Gestapo.

Fifteen minutes later Peter came in to see me. His eyes went instantly to Molly. He gave me one of his inscrutable Peter looks. Then wordlessly he beckoned to her. Happily released from the bondage of crayoning, Molly went. The door closed behind them.

I tried to go back to work but I couldn't stand the suspense. I looked all around the office, but there was no sign of Peter or Molly. Finally, I went in the recording studio. Peter had Molly in the booth and he was recording her reciting nursery rhymes.

"I've decided to start a children's line of audiotapes," he told me. "Starring Molly."

Molly, taking all this totally in stride, continued to recite "Little Boy Blue." I was so moved by the sight of my baby sitting behind the big microphone, doing such a good job, that I started to cry. Molly and Peter both turned around and glared at me. I was ultimately evicted from the room.

March 26

Molly's away with Mitch. I needed to get out of the apartment, so I drove aimlessly around for awhile. Ended up in Hollywood, of all places. Really made a meal of it. Visited Frederick's and Grauman's Chinese Theatre. Went into the Hollywood Wax Museum, and Ripley's Believe It or Not. Gawked at the stars on the Walk of Fame. Things I haven't done since I was eight.

Believe me, it was a lot more fun when I was eight.

Then, driving home, I passed the spot where the Bijou Theatre used to be. And I turned instantly into Proust, eating his madeleine.

Raising My Titanic

The Bijou Theatre—I haven't thought about it in years. But suddenly it was all back, and more real than anything in the present day. For a moment I was a teenager again, with no job, no Cancer of the Month, no electric bill, and Molly just a dream in my future.

It was Buddy who first took me there, one hot August afternoon. He wouldn't tell me where we were going, only said it was a surprise and that I would love it. I was in a grumpy mood that day, and knew I would hate it.

I loved it. The Bijou Theatre was the most wonderful movie house in the world—so tiny that it literally held only ten or twelve seats. It had this weird, freakily decorated lobby, and it showed all the great old films from the thirties and forties.

We saw a double-feature that day. *The Golddiggers of 1933* and another musical. I don't recall the name, but I do remember that Jimmy Cagney was in it, singing a song about lookin' for his Shanghai Lil. It was pure enchantment. I came home and raved so much that Mama declared she wouldn't rest until she, too, had had the Bijou experience. So the next day, Buddy and I took her to see the shows; afterward, we all had hot fudge sundaes at Will Wright's and drove the waitresses crazy, singing about how we were lookin' for our Shanghai Lil.

Well, the Bijou Theatre was torn down years ago and there's no longer a Will Wright's. Jimmy Cagney's dead, and so's Mama.

That makes me so very sad, the passage of time. It feels so eerie and scary, getting older and being able to remember things that are no longer there.

Later

Just talked to Scott. We were talking about getting my closet door fixed, when suddenly I burst into tears and started babbling about days long past. Scott was absolutely wonderful. He said he remembered the Bijou Theatre perfectly; and together we went down the list of Will Wright's ice cream flavors. So I feel much better now. I guess that, as long as I have Scott, I will always have the Bijou and Will Wright's. And lookin' for my Shanghai Lil.

March 28

Well, Cheryl says she's given me a whole month to recover from the Deke disaster—and that it's now time for me to get back into circulation. She wants to give my phone number to this guy she met on the set last week. His name is Rick Bendel. (My first thought, I confess, was "Bendel—as in the chic New York boutique?") But he's got nothing to do with retail. Apparently, he's some Hot Young Studio Executive, and Cheryl thinks we might just hit it off.

Am very suspicious. Part of me thinks that Scott is right, that I've got some inner growing to do before any relationship I get in will work. But another part of me says, hey, what the hell. It beats spending a seventh evening in a row being beaten at Candyland by Molly.

Raising My Titanic

March 30

I should have been warned. I should have been warned the moment Rick Bendel called me up yesterday at work.

"Hello," he said. "This is Rick. Is this Betty?"

I said it was.

"What are you wearing?" he asked me.

"A jade-green sheath," I lied. (Maybe he's Antique Winter, too, and this was some kind of test to see if we're compatible.)

"Sounds good," he went on smoothly. "And what are you wearing underneath it?"

I resisted the urge to hang up in a cold feminist fury. At least give him a chance, I told myself. Maybe he's just one of those guys who aren't very good on the phone.

He said he would pick me up at the apartment. I got carefully dressed, and at six the doorbell rang.

The moment I opened the door, I knew instantly that this whole date was a terrible mistake. He was tall and gangly; I hate tall and gangly. He was red-haired; I hate red-haired. He had a pointy little face and pointy little glasses. All in all, he looked like a Christmas elf gone completely to seed.

Next time I see Cheryl, I will dismember her.

And what was worst of all, I could tell that Rick Bendel was equally unimpressed with me.

Well, we both politely got over our mutual shock, and he suggested going down to Venice, where a friend of his was holding an art show. I said how delightful. An art show in Venice. How Californian. How newly divorced.

It was a freezing night, but I had wanted to look attractive, so I had worn my new skirt and blouse which is gorgeous but skimpy, at best. (Of course, once I got my first look at Rick and realized the whole thing was no go, I should have just grabbed my beat-up old tweed coat; but who can think that fast?) Anyway, we went out to his car. It turned out to be an old, open jeep.

Now this might have charmed me if it had been a hot summer day; or it might even have charmed me tonight, had Rick been dark-haired and devastatingly cute; but it wasn't, and he wasn't—and it was all I could do not to call off the date right then and there.

The drive to Venice was challenging. In the first place, the jeep had a tendency to tip whenever we reached a corner. (This was probably due to the fact that Rick drove at ninety miles an hour.) In the second place, the cold wind that builds up in a jeep going ninety miles an hour is not to be believed. And in the third place, Rick and I grew to hate each other—more than I would have ever dreamed possible on such a short acquaintance. Within five minutes of hearing him brag about his job and his life, I had him

Raising My Titanic

pegged as a shallow, opportunistic climber. And then when I told him about my job and my life, I could see myself being pegged as a stagnant, domestic bore.

We disagreed on every subject we touched upon. Bette Davis films, restaurants, architectural styles, men's hairdos. By the time we reached the gallery, we were no longer speaking.

And the art show was awful. Now—trust me on this—I like art. I like modern art. I took three art history courses at Stanford, and I can throw heavy, intellectual terms around with the best of them. But this show was not about art. It was about a bunch of posturing people pretending to talk about art. They reminded me of my college days—and those snobby kids who went around mourning that there wasn't a decent croissant to be found in the whole San Francisco area.

And then we come to the art itself. How can I do justice to it? I will merely describe one tasty little number. It was a long cardboard tube, painted in green tempera. Its title was "Sick Sperm."

When I laid eyes on this masterpiece I grabbed Rick and told him, in the same tones I use to tell Molly to get her hand out of the garbage disposal, that it was time to go home.

He had had a lot to drink and was in no condition to drive—but I couldn't handle the stick-shift on his jeep. So, feeling in rather a suicidal mood anyway, I took a chance.

Our ride home was memorable. He weaved and wandered

all over the road, while I hung out the window, like an Old West Scout, keeping an eye out for policemen.

Finally he pulled up in front of my apartment building. I sat in the jeep a moment, not knowing quite what to do. My conscience said that Rick was in no shape to drive home alone, and that I could at least offer him some coffee to sober him up. But the rest of me was yelling, "Run for your life!"

Conscience won. I asked Rick in for coffee. The moment the words were out, a look of dawning horror came into his face. He was gone from my driveway almost before I'd had time to get out of the jeep.

My humiliation is total—did he really think I was trying to seduce him?

Have been looking in the mirror. Are things really *that* bad?

March 31

Called up Scott and told him about the evening. He acted very smug and said that he wasn't in the least surprised.

Enjoyed hanging up on him.

Next I called up Cheryl and told her never, never to set me up with anyone unless I saw his photo first. Told her at length about the evening. She said it all sounded like a great adventure, and

that I was ridiculously picky. Asked the price of "Sick Sperm"—
said she might buy it for her hallway.

Enjoyed hanging up on her, too.

April 1

April Fools' Day. Peter played several sweet jokes on me, including calling me up, telling me he was from the AMA, and that my
dentist had been reported as a carrier of AIDS. When I realized
it was Peter on the phone, I blew up. Told him he had finally
gone too far—and that I quit.

Went back to my desk and thought it over. Considered things
like my rent money, and the cost of keeping Molly in crayons,
and how hard it is to get a job. And how dull life would be without Peter.

Went into his office and told him "April fool."

Came home and found Molly bitten by the same evil spirit. She
told me fourteen times that there was a big black spider climbing
up my dress. Thirteen times, it was an April Fools' joke. The
fourteenth time, it was for real. The hairy little devil was making
his way down me like a quarterback on a football field. I ran
around the apartment, shrieking and trying to tear off my dress.
Molly loved every moment. I suspect she planted the spider on
me, but I cannot think how.

Reading this paragraph over, I realize that paranoia is becoming a growing tendency.

April 2

Am really looking forward to this morning. Am taking Molly to the park and we're finally removing the training wheels from her bicycle. A big moment.

I remember so well the day that my training wheels were taken off. I was five years old, on a hot summer's afternoon. Dad and Mama took me to the park, and I was told the surprising and terrifying news that I was about to learn to ride a bicycle all by myself.

Dad took off the training wheels and he pushed me up and down the length of the park, again and again. I pushed wobbly on the pedals, and then suddenly the footsteps stopped and I realized I had left my father far behind me. I looked back and there was Dad, panting, grinning, covered in perspiration; and there was Mama, crying, shouting "Bravo, baby!" and taking pictures. I will never forget that morning.

Later

Feel a little sad. The bicycling didn't go terribly well. We tried for forty-five minutes, but for some reason, we just couldn't do it. Molly couldn't pedal fast enough, and I couldn't hold her up. She just kept crashing down. We left the park before the other kids had a chance to snicker.

Feel I've let Molly down. Feel I've let my Dad down. And I will probably have to pay for the damage done to the water fountain.

April 6

Am in a good and peaceful mood tonight. Getting ready for Easter. It's my favorite holiday—I guess because it's not all balled up with expectations—and so I'm never disappointed.

I love every part of Easter, the spiritual and the temporal both. And I can't tell you how excited I still get over those marshmallow chicks.

LIST OF EASTER MEMORIES

"First Memory"—my fourth. I woke up one morning and found the most wonderful basket on my bed, filled with stickers and lollipops. Mama said it was from the Easter Bunny. I had never heard of the Easter Bunny, and I got it confused with "Esther," our housekeeper. This really amazed me since Esther had always hated me. She used to pull my hair and lock me in the coat closet. And now suddenly here she was, giving me lollipops and stickers. What a miracle. I soon found out my mistake but the impression stuck. And ever since then, Easter for me has not been about Jesus' resurrection, but about Esther's.

"Most Mixed-Blessing Easter"—my seventh. We went to visit my Aunt Becky. She gave me an adorable baby chick. My euphoria lasted exactly two days, and then the chick met a terrible death that I won't go into here, except to say that it involved the vacuum cleaner.

"Most Miraculous Easter"—my eleventh. Dad hadn't worked in a while, and it was one of our lean years. Mama and I went by Saks one day, and we saw this beautiful children's dress in the window—pink-and-white-striped silk with flowers embroidered on the collar. I knew there was no way she could afford to buy it for me. But Easter morning came, and there was the dress on my bed. I still don't know how she managed it.

"Saddest Easter"—my sixteenth. I spent the day with Buddy. We went for a picnic at Will Roger's State Park, and he gave me a little toy lamb. Then at sunset, he took me to the Bel-Sands Hotel in Brentwood. We rode the glass elevator up to the top floor. There was a bar up there, and a dance floor, and a panoramic view.

I found the whole scene depressing and grim. Smog everywhere, and the San Diego Freeway jammed with irritable, sluggish cars.

Buddy tried hard to give me a good time. He asked me to dance but I wasn't in the mood. I finally left him and put my head against the glass window, looking at all those cars. I thought about how trivial and dull life was and how I couldn't wait to grow up.

That sort of ended my happy Easter memories for a while.

Now that I have Molly, though, it's all back. The bunnies and the

R a i s i n g   M y   T i t a n i c

baskets and the pastel colors. And since they're all ostensibly for my little girl, I can enjoy them without anyone knowing. Have already bought three boxes of marshmallow chicks.

April 8

Scott has decided that my education in matters worldly and spiritual is woefully incomplete. So this evening he took me first to a very bizarre religious movie called *The Rapture,* and then afterward to a porno shop. The two were not as unalike as you might think. I guess fanaticism in any form makes its own world with its own rules.

Of the two, however, I confess I lean towards the latter. Seeing *The Rapture* did not make me want to become a born-again Christian, but I tell you, there were some pretty interesting-looking devices in that porno shop. Did not have the nerve, however, to buy anything.

April 10

Easter Sunday. Scott came over with two Easter baskets—one for Molly and one for me. Molly's was filled with every kind of junk food she is ordinarily forbidden to eat, and mine—he made me open it in the privacy of my bathroom—was filled with all the interesting-looking devices I had seen the other night at the porno shop.

I didn't have enough batteries for them all.

April 11

Have come down with an incredibly sore throat, the worst I've ever had. I'm pretty sure it's cancer. My Uncle Neil died of throat cancer, and now I've got it.

My whole life up till now has been so muddled and confusing. And now it's ending.

Later

Took the afternoon off and went to the doctor. He gave me some antibiotics. Cancer seems to be cured.

April 12

Interesting developments. I actually went out on a date tonight. It was all Cheryl's doing, as usual—but this time she showed me the guy's photo first, and I preapproved it.

Raising My Titanic

His name is Dan Franks, and he's the new publicist on her show. On Friday, Cheryl gave him the go-ahead to call me, and he phoned that very afternoon. He couldn't have sounded more courteous or gallant.

And tonight we went out.

First off, he's exceedingly handsome. Not even the kind of quirky handsome where you have to dig a little, but the hit-you-over-the-head kind of handsome that you keep marveling afresh at, every time you see him from a different angle.

And he's had a very intriguing background. He moved to Los Angeles from Germany only last year, and he exudes that European polish, those wonderful courtly mannerisms. He also uses words with many, many syllables. It is definitely good for my ego to spend an evening with someone who is so attractive, smart, and cultured.

Strangely, though, in spite of all these pleasant factors, it wasn't the most fun evening of my life. By the time the date was wearing down, I must admit I was pretty worn down myself. Dan is a talker. Boy, is Dan a talker. But the only thing Dan can talk about is Dan.

LIST OF THINGS DAN TALKS ABOUT

1. How he is the most gifted person in the whole publicity department, and yet is held back by other

people's jealousy of his (a) outstanding looks, (b) enormous talents, (c) I.Q. of 167;

2. How abysmal it is that all the women he's met in Hollywood are only interested in men who have (a) position, (b) wealth, (c) a great car;

3. How, since he has moved to Hollywood last year, he has not yet met a single person who could help him attain (a) position, (b) wealth, (c) a great car;

4. How, in spite of never having been married, he intends to write a book on relationships—one that will sell a million copies. When I asked him why he was sure the book would do so well, he told me he plans to put a color picture of himself on the back cover.

By the time the evening was over, I was pretty exhausted and a little disgusted. This did not, however, prevent me from wanting Dan to kiss me goodnight. When we reached the door to my apartment, I put my face up with just the right amount of shy invitingness—and he kissed me gallantly on the hand.

Went inside, slightly miffed. A nice kiss could have made even the I.Q. of 167 palatable.

Raising My Titanic

April 13

Bought Molly the most adorable dress today. Blue with tiny white flowers, and an organdy pinafore. It cost a fortune, but I whipped out my already overcharged American Express card without a moment's hesitation. I love buying clothes for Molly. I actually start to tremble when I see an outfit that would look cute on her. I spend three times as much money on her wardrobe as I do on my own, but why not? She's three times as cute as I am.

But it makes me sad. She's already into a size 4. Pretty soon she'll be out of the pinafore world entirely.

April 14

Took Molly to church today. She got so involved with the sermon. Every time the minister asked a rhetorical question from the pulpit, her little hand shot up in the air, eager to answer.

Had a nice brunch afterwards, at Hamburger Hamlet. Molly informed me, over her waffle, that she didn't want to be called Molly anymore.

"What do you want to be called?" I asked.

She thought about it a second.

"Freya, Goddess of Love."

· · ·

A wonderful surprise in the afternoon. My beloved Aunt Becky is in town for the day, en route back to Seattle from her cruise in the South Seas. She took Freya and me to the Huntington Gardens for tea. She let Freya eat seven brownies, and when no one was looking, held her up by the heels so she could steal pennies out of the wishing pond.

April 15

Dan Franks called me tonight. He really does have the most extremely attractive voice, pleasant and smooth and manly. Pity the only word he can say with it is "I." Still, this did not prevent me from accepting his invitation to dinner tonight.

Later

Have a few free minutes before Dan arrives. He's picking me up at work—that's good. When he and Molly meet, I want the circumstances to be exactly right.

Have done a lot of thinking today, and I've decided that I've been altogether too hard on Dan. Yes, the guy did talk about himself a lot the other evening; but that was probably just "first-date jitters." By tonight, I bet the conversation will be all about me—where it belongs. And, as far as his not kissing me, that was also probably due to nerves. All in all, feel quite hopeful.

Raising My Titanic

April 16

All in all, feel quite stupid.

Dan came by at six, excited about going to this new restaurant in the Sunset Plaza. I hated the place on sight. It had just been praised in *Los Angeles Magazine,* and was absolutely mobbed by the young Hollywood crowd.

I suggested we leave and come back in a few months, when the restaurant had settled back down to obscurity. But Dan looked so aghast at the suggestion that I pretended it had been a joke.

I took the philosophical approach: How often do I get to go to a crowded restaurant with someone who looks as good as Dan?

The waitress seated us side by side at a front booth. She put Dan on my left, by the window. I guess she thought he would be a good advertisement for the restaurant.

The moment she left I could tell something was wrong. Dan seemed to be getting edgier by the second. You could just feel this palpable tension coming from him. Finally he turned to me and said, "Would you mind if we changed places?"

A horrible, horrible thought popped into my mind. So horrible that I couldn't help blurting it out.

"Dan," I said, "just please tell me this doesn't have something to do with your profile."

And he blushed. I swear, the man blushed.

"Well, yes, it does," he said. "I look better from the right side."

9 5

MARY SHELDON

. . .

In silence, we changed seats.

The evening was a complete embarrassment. Dan was childish, demanding, and rude to the waitress. He complained about the room temperature, the clientele, the service, the music, and he sent back his soup three times. I cringed to be seen with him and kept trying to look like a business associate, not a date. But did all this prevent me from wanting a goodnight kiss when the evening was over? Of course not.

When he dropped me off at my apartment, I asked him in for a cup of tea. I had my strategy all planned out. It was ten o'clock. Molly would be fast asleep, and I would get rid of the baby-sitter inside of three minutes.

I'd brew some tea, and make sure not to give Dan "Sleepytime." We'd sit on the sofa and talk about films. At some point, I'd wangle the conversation around to my favorite movie, *Holiday,* and tell him I'd just gotten a VHS copy.

What? You mean you've never seen *Holiday?* Oh, but you must—immediately! At least a few minutes of it.... Of course, the VCR is in my bedroom, but if you don't mind going in there to watch it....

Well, the minute I opened the apartment door, all plans for seduction faded abruptly away. For there was the baby-sitter, agitated and pleading; and there was Molly, covered in ice

Raising My Titanic

cream, yelling her head off. Not exactly what I wanted Dan's first impression of her to be.

Then, when she saw Dan, Molly stopped dead.

"I think it would be best if you left," she told him politely. "As you can see, Mama has many things to straighten out here."

Dan kissed me swiftly on the cheek and disappeared. I turned around to Molly, ready to kill her. But she was smiling now. She helped me off with my sweater, helped the baby-sitter on with hers, and trotted off obediently to bed.

April 17

Well, Peter is being sued—for the seventh time this year. I had to go into court this morning and do a deposition. I dressed very carefully, in the most Honest-Citizen-looking clothes I own. I must have looked pretty good—one of the officers winked at me as I came in.

What an endless, grueling morning. At noon, it was finally over—I left the courtroom feeling like Numbers 1-5 on the 10 Most Wanted list. But Peter seems strangely unperturbed by the drama. In fact, I think he gets strength from it. By the time he left the courtroom, I swear he looked younger, ruddier, more rested than when he came in. I, on the other hand, looked like a refugee from Shangri-la. The same officer who had winked at me when I came in shuddered in thinly disguised horror when I came out.

April 18

Went to a romantic movie with Dan last night. Bought short skirt for the occasion. He held my hand for a few minutes during the film.

But no goodnight kiss.

April 19

Went for a drive with Dan last night. For two endless hours, I listened sympathetically to his tales of office politics. Was hoping that, as a reward, there would be a kiss. There was no kiss.

April 20

Went to the Moonlight Tango with Dan. He dances very well, if a little too perfectly. Couldn't help but be reminded of a German goose step. He had a glass of wine, and went so far as to tickle my fingers. I was filled with hope. Came home. No kiss.

Very depressed.

Raising My Titanic

Later

Have talked to some friends about the Dan situation, and how to handle it.

1. Pat's advice: That he hasn't kissed me because he respects me and wants to get to know me as a person first. So I should be glad.

2. Sondra's advice: That he's going slow for fear of disease. (How flattering.)

3. Cheryl's advice: Get him inside the apartment, then double-lock the door. Say I won't let him out until he kisses me.

4. Scott's advice: That the whole kissing question is totally immaterial. Dan's obviously the wrong person for me, we'd be a disaster together, so why not face up to that and forget the whole thing right now? Query: Is Scott just being his usual wise, metaphysical self, or does he have secret designs on Dan?

April 21

Unbelievable developments. Dan and I went out tonight. This time I had Molly all prepared. I told her that Mama's new friend was coming and that I would like her to be nice to him—the same way I am to all *her* friends. (This last tidbit I got out of the February issue of *Parents* magazine.) She promised she would try, but added darkly that it would be difficult. She thought Dan looked like Frankenstein's Monster, and she might confuse the two before the night was out.

Dan arrived, and for five minutes he tried very, very hard to "relate" to Molly. He asked her about school, how old she was—all the questions Molly most hates. She shot me killer glances, but true to her promise, remained civil.

But then, just as Dan and I were leaving to go to the restaurant, Molly threw a fit. First, she wailed that she didn't want to be left alone with the baby-sitter (whom she had specifically requested, only that morning). Then she screamed that she was frightened of going to bed, that she had a stomachache and an earache, and that there was a poisoner hiding in the medicine chest. Finally, seeing that none of this was working, she physically attached herself to my leg, and had to be dragged along the hallway like a very attractively dressed cast.

Dan choked that he'd be downstairs waiting for me in the car and made his escape. As the elevator closed behind him, Molly instantly let go of my leg and beamed at me.

Raising My Titanic

"I promised I'd be nice to him," she smirked. "I didn't promise I'd be nice to you."

Somewhat thrown by this scene of domestic hell, I was a little silent on the drive to the restaurant. Dan, with a stunning perceptiveness hitherto unsuspected, actually noticed.

He asked me if anything was wrong.

I amazed myself by my candor.

I told him that, yes, something was wrong—and asked him why he had never once tried to kiss me.

Well, his answer was astonishing. Absolutely astonishing. According to Dan, it's all been my fault. Apparently, I simply haven't been sending out those sort of sexual signals at all. He said my behavior was somewhere between that of Melanie from *Gone with the Wind* and Alice from *Alice in Wonderland*. As both are personal heroines of mine, I don't know whether to be insulted or pleased.

He said that women who want romance let it be known in a variety of subtle ways—all of which have been entirely missing from my behavior.

In a most un-Melanie-like voice I asked him to elaborate.

"Well, if you were really interested, here's what you would do," he told me. "You would invite me over. When I got to your apartment, there would be a note on the front door saying, 'Molly isn't here; I'm all alone and lonely.' And the door would be ajar. I would come in. There would be incense burning, and little arrows pointing to your bedroom. I would go in there, and you would be lying in bed dressed in black lingerie and fishnet stockings. Now *that* would give me the idea."

Can you believe it? Can you believe such a sexist, chauvinistic beast? To think—I've wasted nearly a whole month on this creep. But this is it. No more. Absolutely no more.

April 22

I am devastated. Devastated.

Molly came home from Mitch's last night, sporting a denim miniskirt, sneakers, and a black leather jacket. She looked like a regular at a biker bar. I ripped the clothes off her, and I swear, almost burned them. To my horror, she fought me. She told me that this is the way she wants to dress from now on—and that she especially loves the outfit because "Veronica gave it to her."

I feel like I'm on one of those centrifugal-force rides at carnivals—whirling with such force that I'm pinned helplessly against the wall, and will never move again.

Raising My Titanic

Thoughts on Finding Out That My Ex-Husband Has Found Someone Else

1. What nerve. Imagine not asking my permission before even considering such a move.

2. What sort of idiot, beside myself, would be insane enough to fall in love with Mitch?

3. Maybe he's totally changed since we broke up— maybe he's become the world's most desirable man.

4. Maybe he always was the world's most desirable man, and I just never realized it.

Later

Molly just came in. She was clutching a little piece of paper with Veronica's work number on it.

"Veronica misses me so much when I'm not around," she informed me. "So I think I'd better call her."

I said that Veronica would probably be at lunch now and that a call later in the day would make much more sense. Somehow, though, Veronica's number managed to disappear when Molly next looked for it. And I somehow sense the number will not be found—unless Molly searches the city sewer system.

Later

SECOND THOUGHTS

1. I should be glad Mitch has found happiness. His making a success of his life in no way precludes my having a similar success.

2. I should be grateful that his new girlfriend is kind to Molly.

3. I should be thankful that Molly has a broad variety of friends and influences in her life; she'll grow up to be a much more subtle and substantial person.

Oh, let's cut out the hypocrisy. I'm not glad about any of these things. I'm furious. And I'm terrified. What's going to happen now? Are her little-girl days over so soon? Are my days of influence over so soon? Will Molly want to leave me and move in with Mitch and Veronica?

All day long I kept hearing more. How Veronica lets Molly stay up until ten at night. How Veronica lets her watch all the television she wants. How Veronica lets her have six Oreos. How Veronica doesn't make her brush her teeth.

You want to know what pain is? This is pain.

Raising My Titanic

April 23

No, that wasn't pain. *This* is pain. Tonight was Molly's night to be with Mitch. I was home, editing a script for Peter, when the phone rang. It was Molly, calling from Mitch's car phone.

"Mama!" she said triumphantly. "Good news! I just wanted you to know that Veronica likes the new shoes you bought me!" The relief and joy in her voice nearly killed me. She wanted to keep talking, but from behind her, I could hear a woman's voice. "That's enough dear. It's time to hang up."

And then Mitch's voice, "Get back on Veronica's lap, Molly."

We went through the whole evening together, me and my vision. Molly on Veronica's lap. Molly on Veronica's lap as I ate my scrambled eggs. Molly on Veronica's lap as I watched the news. Molly on Veronica's lap as I tried to get to sleep.

And yet, when I bring a man home, Molly can't even be civil. Is this some sort of cosmic punishment being dealt out to me? Or does Molly just have better taste than I do?

April 24

I cannot believe what I did today. I must be ill—very seriously ill. I called Dan Franks. I called him and told him to come over at six o'clock tonight.

When he came, there was a note on the door, saying that Molly was playing at her friend Twyla's house, and that I was alone. There was incense burning in the foyer, and a bunch of little arrows, scotch-taped to the walls. The arrows stopped at the bedroom door. And when Dan opened the bedroom door, there I was on the bed, wearing black lingerie and fishnet stockings.

And what did he do? He laughed. He laughed and he laughed. He said I was the cutest thing in the world, then he came over, kissed me on the cheek, and fled. For several minutes, I sat there on the bed, torn, as the bad novels say, between laughter and tears.

Then the doorbell rang. I jumped up, thinking Dan had changed his mind, and was coming back to ravish me. I flung open the door. Outside was Molly, returning home from Twyla's house. When she saw me, her little face lit up. "Why, Mama," she said. "You look just like Veronica!"

Raising My Titanic

April 25

I'm so excited. Peter called me into his office this morning, with a strange little smile on his face. He asked me if I knew who Elliot Frobisher was. I laughed and told him that everyone knew who Elliot Frobisher was, then added modestly that maybe I knew a little more about him than most, since I had done a monologue from his play *Shipwreck* in the tenth grade, and had won the talent show because of it. I would have been more than happy to go into the monologue, but Peter interrupted.

"Great," he said, "then you're perfect for the job."

I asked him what job.

He told me that he had just gotten off the phone with Elliot Frobisher's agent. Apparently, Frobisher plans on coming out with some essays on audio—his first in years—and he wants Bookworm to bring the tape out. The weird little smile reappeared.

"And I'm letting you produce it."

God Bless Peter. This is the biggest thing I've ever done professionally. We're talking possible Spoken Word Grammy here.

Later

Was too excited to eat lunch. Went to the library instead and checked out everything I could find about Frobisher—his plays, essays, and the three unauthorized biographies that have been written about him. Have been racing gluttonously through them. What a strange and romantic guy. Living incognito on some unidentified island, giving no interviews, doing no publicity. Even his publisher isn't sure what he looks like.

Have been having all kinds of wonderful fantasies. The two of us meet, over this project. I do the monologue for him. He senses immediately that I understand his work as no one has ever understood it before. He coaxes me into leaving Bookworm. I do not need much coaxing. For kindness's sake, I finish the tape, pocket my Spoken Word Grammy, and go with Elliot back to his unidentified island. Our relationship is not based on romance: First, he is a bony and disfigured ascetic and second, after the Dan fiasco, I've had it with men—but we live in peace and creative fulfillment together. There are excellent schools on the unidentified island, and Molly has her own fishing boat.

I love it. God Bless you, Peter. God Bless you.

April 26

Peter, you double-dyed devil. Now I understand why you gave this project to me.

There is something they do not tell you in tenth grade English class. Nor in the three unauthorized biographies. Elliot Frobisher is completely insane.

For the last twenty-four hours, I have been trying to get hold

Raising My Titanic

of him, to discuss the project. He never gave Peter a number where he could be reached, so I have left five messages at his agent's office. But all the receptionist will say is that Mr. Frobisher will be in contact with me when he wishes.

Then, today at work, a fax came sliding through my machine. On it were Elliot Frobisher's dictums.

He will not talk on the phone. He will not answer a fax. He will not come in for a meeting. He will not give me a typescript of the essays. He will not give me even a rough idea of what they will be about. And he will especially not come into the recording studio to read them.

Here is what he is willing to do. He is willing to call my apartment, on three unannounced occasions, and recite the essays extemporaneously onto my telephone answering machine.

April 27

Am a nervous wreck. I have bought the best, most reliable, and most expensive answering machine in town. I then bought a second answering machine for the bedroom phone, in case the first one breaks down. When I asked Peter if he would like to chip in for these purchases, he laughed heartily. I check these two answering machines ten times a day, to make sure they're still working. But what if, on the big Elliot Frobisher nights, they don't work? What if I forget to turn them on? What if there's a power outage? What if Molly gets up in the middle of the night and answers the phone? What if Frobisher dials a wrong number and gets someone else's machine? One of the great essays of modern literature could be lost forever. Not to mention my job.

April 28

Today's my birthday. It is just not possible that I am thirty-one years old.

Ten years ago, age meant absolutely nothing. I would look at my little unlined face in the dorm room mirror and wonder what all the fuss over staying young was about. Okay, so I didn't have the body and face I had had when I was sixteen. But I thought that, all things considered, I was aging pretty gracefully.

And even five years ago, age didn't mean that much. I was married, I was expecting a baby—I was safe. Mitch had long since stopped noticing what I looked like, and all babies think their mothers are beautiful, even if the mothers look like Agnes the Goon.

But today I am standing in front of the mirror looking like Agnes the Goon and Molly is standing behind me, this queer look on her face.

"I think you'd better get a haircut," she tells me dubiously. "Or *something*."

·   ·   ·

Raising My Titanic

To cheer myself up, I believe I'll retreat to the past.

List of Great Birthdays

Best Loot Birthday—my eighth. My father hadn't worked in over a year. Then right before my birthday, the studio bought his "Biker Zombies from Hell" idea. Mama went into present-buying overdrive. That was the birthday of the bicycle and the fish tank and the fourteen Madame Alexander dolls.

Biggest Surprise Birthday—my twelfth. Mama picked me up from school, looking very grim and no-nonsense. She told me that I had a dentist's appointment scheduled. We drove toward Dr. Marcus's office—and then she looked down at her dashboard and gasped that the car was overheating. We were near Will Wright's, and she pulled into the parking lot. She told me to stay in the car and that she would use their phone to call the Auto Club. "No, I can't leave you in the car alone—you'd better come in with me," she sighed.

The moment we walked in Will Wright's, the whole restaurant seemed to explode with "Surprise!" There were all my friends, sitting at tables, grinning at me and singing "Happy Birthday!" I was so stunned—and so mad at Mama because I was still in my school uniform, and there was ink on my face.

Happiest Birthday—my sixteenth. Funny that this one should come to mind. It was really so low-key. Mama and Dad and Buddy and I went to see *Citizen Kane* at the Bijou Theatre, and then on to Hamburger Hamlet afterwards. Toward the end of the dinner, Dad pointed above my head and said, "Look at this poster!" It was a poster of John Barrymore playing Hamlet, and Dad started telling me all about his performance. It was only meant to be a ruse, so that I would turn my back, and not see the waitress bringing my birthday cake to the table—but what Dad had to say about John Barrymore was so interesting that everyone, including the waitress, got so caught up in his story that they forgot to start singing "Happy Birthday."

That was also the night I got the beautiful green taffeta dress from Mama and Dad; and Buddy gave me a gold heart for my charm bracelet. I remember feeling so tremendously cherished and so tremendously happy.

And finally, we have:

Worst Birthday—Today. Molly woke me at five-thirty in the morning, proudly carrying in a beautiful handmade birthday card. I exclaimed over it so much that she changed her mind about giving it away, and ended up keeping it herself.

Then I got into work, and was cheered to find a small, prettily wrapped package on my desk. I opened it. It was a gift from Peter: a fourteen-carat gold necklace with the letters *B-I-T-C-H* hanging from it.

Then Cheryl brought over her offering. Along (admittedly) with a lovely peach silk dress, came a card that showed a teacher standing in front of a classroom saying, "Class, we will now conjugate the verb *Old:* I am old. You is old. He, she and it is old." And then, on the inside, *"We is all old."*

Raising My Titanic

Like a catchy tune, this little jingle stayed in my head all morning long. By lunchtime, I felt like I was a hundred. *We is all old.* It took me twenty minutes to shuffle, crooked-backed, down the street. Scott took me to La Scala, to celebrate my having lived so long. Ordered a chocolate-nut cake for dessert—broke a front cap on a walnut shell.

Is this what life at thirty-one is like?

April 30

Life at thirty-one has improved. Last night I was sitting watching a horror movie with Molly, when there was a whir from the answering machine. Onto it came the most ironic and most attractive male voice. "This is Elliot Frobisher...." he began. I scuttled around with the panic of a snake deprived of its rock; but both answering machines were trusty and true. I turned off the movie and sat there in Heaven, listening to the essay. What a piece of work. So intelligent and subtle. The almost-musical linkage of themes. The mordant humor. I think I'll revise the fantasy a little. Maybe I won't make Elliot Frobisher a bony, disfigured ascetic anymore.

When the essay was over, the instant Frobisher finished talking, I lunged for the phone, hoping I could speak with him. But the line went dead.

Molly was staring at me with real concern.

"You turned off *Attack of the Crab Monsters* for that?"

May 1

Today was a very strange day. I went to a bridal shower. It was for Amy Matthews, the daughter of one of Daddy's old directors. It was held at the Bel Air Country Club—how beautiful that place is. It reminded me of everything I never quite became, everything I think my father secretly always wanted me to be. The debutante in the tulle dress, drinking iced tea.

I am ashamed to say it, but I felt very jealous of Amy today. I was ten when she was born, and I remember going over to her house, the day she was brought home from the hospital. I couldn't for the life of me see why everyone was making such a fuss over this little red-faced baby. To me, she was a lot less interesting than my Siamese cats. I was in the prime of my life then: best student in the fifth grade, best handball player in the class, and three boys had sent me Valentines signed with *love*. I was very hot stuff, and Amy was only an ugly infant.

And now, it's twenty-one years later, and I'm no longer the star of the fifth grade. I've lost a lot of the people that made my life wonderful, and I'm very aware of how precarious and precious it all is.

And here's Amy: twenty-one years old, beautiful, on the verge of everything, and so confident. You just know that she'll never have a boss like Peter. You just know that she'll never have a husband like Mitch.

Raising My Titanic

.　　.　　.

She was very kind to me today, went out of her way not to treat me like I was in her parents' generation. She introduced me to all her friends, who were also very kind and interested. They all seemed fascinated by my job—what I did, and what stars I met. It occurred to me, uncomfortably, that all these bright young college women would, in a year or two, be looking for jobs themselves; I only hoped they didn't go after mine. Because I got the distinctly ominous feeling that any one of them could probably do it a lot better than I do.

After lunch, Randy, Amy's fiancé, came by to watch her open her presents. What a thoroughly decent, sweet young man. The way he looked at Amy. I wanted to cry.

I couldn't help thinking of my own wedding shower. Not one of my gladder memories. Dad had died not very long before, and everything was still pretty subdued. Things weren't wonderful financially, but Mama managed to put together a little afternoon party for my friends.

I came upon her, right before the shower, and found her crying on her bed. She told me she was just tired and I wanted to believe that. I don't know what she was really crying about. Daddy not being there or maybe just the fear of losing her daughter. Or maybe it was that I was marrying Mitch.

Well, I wish Amy every happiness. But I left the shower early and went home.

May 5

Two in the morning. Got a call. Peter's checked himself into the hospital. An emergency. Wants me to come over right away. I panic. Picture Peter near death, and start blubbering like an idiot. I dress in two minutes—but what to do with Molly? I can't call the baby-sitter up at this time of night—so have no other choice. Wake up the sleepy little thing, put her in her robe, and take her with me.

Drive crazily to the hospital. Park expensively. Then, as I walk in the door, I feel myself instantly contracting every contagious disease there. Doubt if I'll make it out of the building alive. Finally find Peter's floor. The nurse, very nice, offers to baby-sit Molly for a few minutes, and gives me directions on how to get to Peter's room. But I'm so paranoid about hospitals that I can't even raise my eyes from the floor; I end up taking the wrong turn. Find myself back at the nurse's desk. This time Molly comes with me as a guide.

Peter in bed, looking extremely Grecian in the hospital robe. No tubes up his nose, no drips in his arm. Only magazines and faxes covering the bed. He glares at me when I come in. Tells me what a terrible mother I am for having brought Molly, says this experience will doubtless scar her for life. Then he puts her on top of his bed and has her practice her reading on his faxes.

I ask what exactly he's in the hospital for. Airily, he waves his hand. Stress, he explains—but he'll be out of there in twenty-four

Raising My Titanic

hours. In the meantime, though, there are a few dozen things that need to be taken care of at the office. With a sweet smile, he hands me a yellow pad on which to take notes.

I look at the large roll of surgical gauze sitting on the bedside table. If I wrapped it around his neck and strangled him, how many years in jail would that get me? But the thought of my responsibility to Molly stays my hand.

"Peter," she's saying, still reading the faxes, "what does this word mean?"

She shows him the word—I could only guess as to what it might be—and Peter coughs.

"I'm sure it's a misspelling," he says. Then he sighs, looks at me pityingly, and shakes his head. "You don't get enough sleep," he tells me.

Later

My pain is appeased. I came home from work today, and the light on the answering machine was blinking. I pushed the retrieval button, and lo: that deep ironic voice I live for.

Elliot Frobisher calling in his second essay. If anything, it's better than the first—makes me feel intelligent and cultured and pleased with myself, just listening to it.

Perhaps I will wear my peach silk when I accept my Spoken Word Grammy.

May 6

Cheryl has a new boyfriend. Sam, the most talented uncast actor west of the Rockies—or so Cheryl assures me. They met at Dove Restaurant, where, while he waits for his big break, he also waits tables.

I have met this Sam, and I find him self-centered, moronic, a user, and madly handsome. In other words, it's the usual story.

Also find it's the usual story with Cheryl. Since Sam came into the picture, she has lost interest in me completely. Sam has become Rome, with all conversational roads leading directly to him. It is getting old fast.

May 11

Quite a Mother's Day.

Molly came bouncing into my bedroom early this morning, carrying her school satchel. Proudly, she drew from it a rolled-up scroll of colored paper, tied with a ribbon.

"Happy Mother's Day!" she beamed.

I unrolled the scroll and burst into tears of joy. On it was a carefully written and beautifully decorated little list: "I love Mama because …" She wrote that she loves me because I take her to McDonald's. She loves me because I look like a jewel. She loves me because I read to her at night. She loves me because I'm good to her toy cats.

Raising My Titanic

I was so happy to get this list—just so happy. And then, I happened to look over at her knapsack, and I saw a second scroll. This was just too wonderful to bear. Was the list of reasons to love me really that long?

"Another one?" I squealed.

Instantly, her face clouded over.

"No, no," she blurted out, quickly taking the second scroll and putting it behind her back. "This one is for Veronica."

Later

Called Scott for comfort. No comfort. He chewed me out, saying that I must stop getting rocked by every little thing—that I have to learn to be strong and complete within myself. That I mustn't make Molly such a focus in my life. That I must get some personal goals going, and stick to those. And that way, if I'm not leaning, no one can let me down.

Hung up on him.

List of Personal Goals

1. Have a great success with the Elliot Frobisher project.

2. Be given a Spoken Word Grammy for the above.

3. Get back in touch with all old college friends.

4. Take a class in bookbinding.

5. Become intensely spiritual.

6. Learn to play the harp.

7. Read *War and Peace.*

I feel better already.

I wonder what was on Veronica's list.

May 14

Scott came over last night, to take Molly and me to dinner. He brought me a Brahms CD and apologized for being so unsympathetic the other night. He said he hadn't been feeling too well and that my call had upset him. "Never doubt how much I love you," he told me. "I just get a little frantic when you get stupid."

Had to laugh.

Went to Ed Debevic's. Had a great time. Molly loved the fifties atmosphere and the costumed waitresses and has been making pointed inquiries ever since about how one goes about getting a beehive hairdo. We used quarter after quarter on the jukebox, the biorhythm machine, and finding out which of us had the highest rating on the love meter. (Molly.)

Raising My Titanic

It's so touching, how much she adores Scott. The way she always wants to sit next to him, and order exactly what he orders. And how she laughs so hard at his jokes—even the ones I know she's too young to understand.

As we left the restaurant, I noticed our shadows on the ground. Me on the left, and next to me, Scott, and Molly asleep in his arms. The perfect happy little shadow family.

Why can't Molly behave with my dates the way she behaves with Scott?

Why does Scott have to be gay?

Why can't they find a cure for this damned disease?

When will I stop obsessing over when the right guy will come along?

When will the right guy come along?

May 15

Had the best time last night. I took Molly to dinner at McDonald's; and after she fell asleep, I got in bed and reread my favorite bits from *Emma*. At ten, I fixed myself a tray of tea and cookies. Really did the experience up proud. Instead of a Lipton's tea bag, I used the expensive Fortum and Mason tea Cheryl got me for Christmas. *And* I put it in the Wedgewood teapot Mama gave me. *And* I made sure the cookies were Mallomars.

I have to admit it. It was a much more fun evening than most of the dates I've gone on. An awful thought. Am I getting too used to being on my own? Am I getting too jaded now to fall in love again? God. I'm getting old fast.

Tuesday

Talked to Aunt Becky this evening. Told her how my life was going, and she suggested that I move up to Seattle. I said I couldn't possibly. Then she asked me the most horrible question—what I was staying in Los Angeles for.

Have been haunted by this question ever since. My parents are both gone, most of my friends have moved away. The air gets smoggier, the streets get meaner, and the pressure gets worse every day.

Am I thinking about moving? Never. Never.

I can't believe I'm thinking about moving.

May 19

Sorry if this entry is a little incoherent. I'm still feeling the effects of the Valium.

At eight o'clock tonight, I was in the kitchen. Molly was in the den, watching television. The phone rang. Molly picked it up. I didn't think much about it until I heard her say, "Last time you

Raising My Titanic

called, I had to stop watching *Attack of the Crab Monsters,* and now I'm in the middle of my favorite *I Love Lucy*. Would you mind calling back another time?"

With a terrible cry, I zoomed in from the kitchen—but Elliot Frobisher had hung up.

I was very calm. I did not spank Molly. I did not shout at her. I did not tell her she had just destroyed my one and only chance for a Spoken Word Grammy. I did not tell her that I would undoubtedly be fired from my job.

May 20

I have been fired.

Later

The Clara Zeitman tape has to be totally remastered—and fast. I have been rehired.

Later

Feel so terrible over the Frobisher business. I must get hold of that essay. I must. Perhaps if I wrote to him—or flew up to his unidentified island?

Later

Can't believe it. Came home tonight—Molly was with the baby-sitter. I asked her if there'd been any calls. She said "That man called again. He said he was sorry for calling during *I Love Lucy*, and that, if I wasn't watching any show at the moment, could he please leave a message. I told him he could."

Raced to the phone. Nirvana. The best Elliot Frobisher tape yet. Life is wonderful.

May 24

Or again, maybe not. Cheryl's completely flipped. She called me today—apparently, the new romance with Sam the Waiter is on a downhill slide. I'm not surprised. I've seen Cheryl through many relationships, and they all follow basically the same pattern.

In the first few weeks after she meets a guy, she goes into what I call "Cheryl Mode I." That's the "he's different from any other man I've ever met, he's sensitive, he's just misunderstood, that's all" motif. Then, around the fourth week, she starts to slip into the "Cheryl Mode II." That's the "he's starting to act suspiciously, he's cooling towards me, I think he's seeing someone else...." phase.

Usually, Cheryl Mode II ends with a fiery confrontation,

Raising My Titanic

followed by the equally fiery end of the relationship. But I guess this pattern's gotten a little tedious, even for Cheryl. So this time she's decided to add a little novelty to the climactic scene.

And I am to be that little novelty.

The plan is that I will go into Dove one night this week, heavily disguised in a blonde wig. I will go up to Sam at some point during the evening and start flirting outrageously. He will flirt outrageously back with me. Then Cheryl, also heavily disguised, will spring out from a nearby table where she has been sitting, watching the action, and the dramatic confrontation will begin.

The fact that this little scene bears unmistakable resemblances to my favorite *I Love Lucy* episode does not daunt Cheryl in the least. She is an actress, not a writer, and does not mind a little plagiarism.

I cannot believe I agreed to this insanity, but I did.

My Reasons

1. It will be satisfying to unmask Sam for the slimy character he is.

2. Since starring as Blanche in a high school production of *Streetcar,* I haven't had the chance to exercise my dramatic abilities.

3. I'm looking forward to wearing the blonde wig.

May 27

Well, my self-esteem is at an all-time low. Went to Dove as planned. Disguise was perfection. Went up to Sam while he was on his break. Flirted enormously. And there was Cheryl sitting at her table, waiting to spring the moment he started to flirt back. But he didn't flirt back.

I flirted some more. He still didn't flirt back. I flirted desperately, my whole ego as a woman on the line. He threatened to have me turned out of the restaurant.

Slunk out. Cheryl slunk out right after me. In silence, we walked the pavement of Sunset Plaza together.

"Maybe he was faking," she finally said. "Maybe he recognized you all the time."

Maybe I'm just not meant to be a blonde.

June 1

Work is beyond crazy. I suspect that the purpose of Peter's new goatee is to make his resemblance to Simon Legree totally complete.

Morale is low. He's working us to death. Someone in the office came up with the idea that we should ask for Flag Day off—and get a little, much-needed rest. But Peter went berserk at the very suggestion.

Raising My Titanic

So naturally, since Flag Day has been denied us, we're all combing the calender to find alternate ways of escape. The 29th is a bank holiday in Britain—so all those with even a drop of English blood are lobbying for release. And then we have St. Jean Baptiste Day in Canada (Shari, who has a grandmother living in Ottawa, plans on taking this one off) and of course there is always the Japanese Constitutional Memorial Day. None of us can pass too easily for Japanese, but May from Vietnam says she's going to try her damndest.

As for me, I'm at the point where misery crosses the line into black comedy. I'm overworked, hysterical, way behind schedule. This morning, I was flipping through my book, *Meditations for Women Who Do Too Much,* and in my rush managed to rip a page right in two.

By the time I get home to Molly, I'm like a character from a Stephen King movie; and she of course proceeds to mirror me faithfully. (Of course, she acts that way when I'm *not* a character from a Stephen King movie too, but that's another story.)

Tonight I told her she had to wash her hair—it was looking like a roadkill. She began the usual ranting and wailing and fussing and complaining.

I said, "Molly, I'm in no mood for theatrics. Let's just get this done without any drama."

The tears stopped instantly. Hurt to the quick, she drew herself up.

"You forget, Mama," she informed me with icy dignity, "that drama happens to be my specialty."

June 2

Well what does work matter anyway? Cancer of the Month has come upon me. Without going into the grisly details, let it suffice to say that these poor old bowels, they ain't what they used to be. In fact, according to the Medical Dictionary, with which I spent an enlightening lunch hour today, I'll be lucky if I last out the week.

Later

Incredible news. Scott called tonight. He's also been feeling stressed-out, and has decided to take a week off and go on a cruise, starting at Acapulco and traveling to the Panama Canal and back. His doctor advised against it, but Scott says he's doing it anyway.

"But are you sure you'll be okay going alone?" I asked anxiously.

"Oh, I'm not going alone," Scott told me. "I'm taking you."

The fantasies run riot. Sun-baked decks! Tropical adventures! A new bikini! Being serenaded by mariachi bands while sipping margaritas!

The very thought of this trip has totally cured my colon cancer.

Raising My Titanic

I'm crazed, desperate. I'll die if I can't go. Especially since Molly will be with Mitch for the last week of June anyway.

But how can I ever do it? Peter won't even give us Flag Day off.

June 5

I can't believe it. I went into Peter's office this morning, and asked him in a faint voice if I could have some vacation time at the end of the month, to go on a cruise. He smiled and said he thought that was a wonderful idea.

Am in total shock. Have I been totally wrong about Peter all this time? Underneath that manic, bullying bluster, could there be lurking a caring, kind, and understanding human being?

Later

The answer is *no*. Am so outraged I can barely type this. Right before lunch, Peter the Caring, Kind, and Understanding came into my office. He was wheeling this enormous UPS cart, the size of a hospital gurney. It was absolutely overflowing with files.

"This cruise idea is a godsend," he told me cheerfully. "You'll be away from all the pressures of the office—and this way, you can get some real work done on the Gottfried deal."

Spent my lunch hour drafting my resignation letter.

. . .

At two o'clock, there was a knock on my door. A delivery from Gucci—addressed to me. It was luggage. The most beautiful, sumptuous, extravagant luggage I've ever seen.

Peter followed the delivery in.

"I got you these so you'll have something to carry the Gottfried reports in," he told me defensively. "I don't want my company to look cheap."

I pointed to the garment bag and the makeup case, and said that I'd have a hard time carrying any reports in those.

Peter blushed a fiery dragon-red.

"I must have ordered those two bags by mistake," he muttered. "But as long as they're here, you might as well keep them."

He fled the room.

Tore up resignation letter.

June 6

Father's Day. Molly spent it with Mitch. She came home this morning, very excited. Veronica had taken her shopping, and the two of them had picked out a present for Mitch together. One of those $5.99 plastic statues that say "World's Greatest Dad."

Got quite tired hearing about the glories of this statue. Finally I dragged out my old college text, "Jansson's History of Art," and showed Molly some *real* statues—the David, the Pietà, Winged Victory. But she stubbornly maintained that none of them could hold a candle to "World's Greatest Dad."

Raising My Titanic

She also mentioned the buying of a plaid shirt. This made me snicker inside. If there's one thing Mitch is never, never going to wear, it's a plaid shirt. Dear Veronica still has a little to learn.

Later

Mitch came by tonight, to drop off the tennis shoe Molly had left at his place. I must say, the plaid shirt looked very nice.

June 9

Today was Amy Matthews's wedding. It was held at her parents' house in Bel Air, a big beautiful home with a tiny stream running through the front yard. It reminded me of the house we lived in when I was five—the year Dad produced *Heart of Fear*.

It's ironic, the way Hollywood works. Sam Matthews never had a tenth of my father's vision or talent, and yet he got the big house with the pool and the tennis court, while Dad wound up in a little apartment in Westwood.

I didn't really feel like mingling with the other guests, so I spent a lot of time wandering around the house. Was pleased to see a big photo of Dad in the library. He had been given a spot on the mantelpiece, and a Tiffany frame.

As it turned out, I knew quite a few people at the party. Old friends of the family, cameramen, a TV director or two, the Sykes, the Fergusons. Realized that, eight years ago, this same group of people had all been collected together for *my* wedding.

A very weird thought.

The ceremony was beautiful and touching. Was filled with such conflicting emotions that the only way I could cope was by eating every miniature quiche on the buffet table.

God, I hate weddings.

June 14

A morning I will never forget. Molly's graduation from preschool. And it's lucky that I'll never forget it—I was trembling so much that the hour and a half of videotape I took didn't come out.

Seeing that little girl marching down the aisle with her class, wearing her tiny cap and gown. Seeing her solemn little face reciting the Pledge of Allegiance. It was just—no. I can't even describe it.

I played a game with myself. I pretended that I had never seen any of these children before, and that I was allowed to choose any of them I wanted for my own.

I chose Molly.

After the ceremony, little yearbooks were handed out. I turned to the literary page, and there was one of Molly's stories—the one about Tweet, the Vampire Parakeet. Can't imagine why they

Raising My Titanic

didn't also include her Thanksgiving story about the homeless turkey bum. That, I think, is her masterpiece.

And on the "Graduates" page, there was her picture, absolutely beautiful. Underneath, it said, "Most Likely to End up on Broadway." I can see myself, in twenty years, when Molly has just won her first Tony Award, giving cute little interviews to *Time* magazine, citing this preschool yearbook prediction. Have made forty copies of the page, one for everyone at the office, and a few extras for the folks at *Time*.

When we got home, Molly asked me if I had ever gotten a yearbook. I said yes, two—one from high school, one from Stanford. The college one I'd lost years ago, but I pulled out my high school yearbook and showed it to her.

Turned out to be a pretty poignant experience, seeing those pictures of my old self. Me in the big draggly sports sweater I was so proud of. Me in the girls' chorus. Me in a rehearsal for Jean Anouihl's *Antigone.* God, I was good in that. In fact, why did I never become a Tony Award–winning actress myself?

But, as it turned out, Molly wasn't very interested in the pictures of me. She preferred seeing the photos of my old classmates, and went down every row, saying, "ugly, cute, pretty, yuck." She didn't think Diana Elliot, the Prom Queen, was pretty at all, but she liked Sharon Aker's looks. (Can you believe it? *Nobody* liked Sharon Aker's looks!) And to my utter horror, she thought Judy Loeb was beautiful. I told Molly that Judy Loeb had been my archrival all through high school, and that she simply wasn't allowed to think she was beautiful.

Then suddenly she said, "Who's that?" I looked down, and saw that she was pointing to a picture of Buddy.

I had forgotten there was even a picture of Buddy in the yearbook. It must have been taken the day our Tuesday Night Drama Group did a scene for my school assembly.

It was a shock, seeing his face again.

By this time, I was feeling pretty emotional anyway and I didn't trust myself to tell Molly a whole lot about Buddy. I merely said that he had been a very special friend of mine.

"Was he your boyfriend?" she pursued.

I said that, yes, in a way, I guess he had been.

Molly stared at me.

"That dreamboat was your *boyfriend*?"

I was slightly miffed by the very unflattering surprise in her voice.

"As a matter of fact," I informed her, "he wanted to marry me."

She considered this.

"So why didn't you marry him?"

I also considered.

"Because there are some men you love and trust and have fun with—and then there are those you marry."

Mercifully, she dropped the subject after that.

Raising My Titanic

June 19

Crazed squared, as I try to get everything in the office organized before I leave for the cruise. I'm dangerously excited. Have fantasies of jumping off the ship and spending the rest of my life as a beachcomber. Then I'll appear later in Molly's life, bohemian and uncouth, à la the convict in *Great Expectations.* and she'll be ashamed of me. But I won't care, because I'll be so gone on kahlua.

I am immersing myself in the preparations. Utterly delicious. Instead of cluttering my computer with details of the Gottfried deal, I fill it with long lists of what clothes I'll need, and what books to bring. Instead of spending lunch hours trying to make sense of the Speight account, I try to make sense of the swimsuit department at Macy's.

This trip will be heaven—pure relaxation, pure fun. I'll come back tanned, calm, able to see the humor in everything. My split ends will all be fused together. And, how's this for insane optimism? Maybe the world's most wonderful man will be by my side.

Later

Speaking of the world's most wonderful man, Scott just came over to organize the final details of the trip. He's got a terrible cough. I really hope this trip's a good idea.

June 22

We leave tomorrow. Took Molly over to Mitch's tonight. I won't see her for eight days. It'll be the longest time I've ever been separated from her. She was very cool about it all. When I told her how much I'd miss her, she only said, "Oh, Mama, it's no big deal. You'll see me in a week."

Dropped her off and came home to find traces of her everywhere. Her little sock with the hole in it. Her scraggly old bunny. Her hairbrush with a few strands of tangled blonde hair. Her scent on the pillow. Had a long, weepy cry. Was roused by the sound of the phone ringing. It was Molly, calling to tell me that my favorite *I Love Lucy* episode was on Channel 11, and she wanted me to know. It sounded as if there was a little tremble in her voice.

June 23

Day 1 of Trip

5:00 A.M. Wake up. Go through list of things I have to do before I can leave. Do all twenty-three things.

Wonder if I've packed everything. Completely unpack suitcase

Raising My Titanic

to check. Discover that packing four days before the trip was not such a good idea. All dresses completely wrinkled. Take them out and iron them.

10:00 A.M. Scott is due. Scott does not come.

10:15. Scott still does not come. I panic.

10:35. Scott arrives. Says there is no cause for alarm, that there is no traffic this time of day.

10:55. Scott is wrong.

11:40. Arrive at airport. Seek signs for long-term parking.

11:50. Find long-term parking. The idea is simple. We park our car in the lot, we carry our bags to a shuttle-bus stop. The bus picks us up, and takes us to our airline terminal.

12 o'clock. Scott and I lug the two-ton bags, doing relays between car and shuttle-bus stop. Shuttle bus comes while we are in mid-relay. Drives on without us. See sadistic smile on face of driver.

12:15. Stranded at bus stop. Check watch every ten seconds.

12:30. Next shuttle bus arrives. Have exactly five minutes to get to the terminal, check bags, go through security, find gate, and board plane. Realize the mathematical impossibility of this. Keep a brave face on things nonetheless.

12:45. Mathematical impossibility borne out. Plane should be gone. But plane is not gone. Am not as rapturous about this news as one might think. Plane has been delayed because of engine trouble.

2 o'clock. Board plane. Sit. Begin stack of work on the Gottfried project.

3 o'clock. Still sitting. Men with anxious faces move back and

forth from the plane. Ditto hydraulic lifts. Then pilot comes on the loudspeaker. Says there is problem with the landing gear. Another two-hour delay. I stand up. Announce dramatically to Scott that the plane is a death trap and that I am not going to fly on it.

3:15. Scott calms me down.

3:17. Pilot comes back on the loudspeaker. Something has now gone wrong with the pressure system. I leap to my feet again. This time, Scott is not able to calm me down.

3:20. We leave the plane.

3:30. Back in the terminal. I fortify myself with a double martini. Scott talks to various airline representatives. Largely, I suspect, because of his great beauty, we are given seats on another airline. It is due to take off in twenty minutes. Our luggage, it is promised, will be waiting for us in Acapulco.

4 o'clock. We board new plane. Plane takes off. I feel effects of double martini. Do not weep and pray as is my normal in-flight behavior. Giggle a great deal. Scott moves to another row. Continue work on the Gottfried account, but am doubtful as to the quality of my efforts.

7 o'clock. Land in Acapulco. Go to find luggage. Luggage is not there.

7:30. Have tracer put on luggage. Luggage is traced. To Brazil.

8 o'clock. Courteous airport officials escort us to a taxi. Assure us that luggage will arrive in the morning. Once again, put courteous behavior down to extreme beauty of Scott.

8:30. Arrive at hotel. It does not look like the pictures in the brochure. Still, am thrilled to be here. Would be even more thrilled

Raising My Titanic

if I had a dress to change into, new underwear, my nightgown and my toothbrush.

9 o'clock. Have dinner in the coffee shop.

9:30. Dinner proves to be bad mistake. Dying so far from home is not a pleasant thought.

Day 2

4 A.M. Find, to my surprise, that I have lived through the night. Watch the Mexican sunrise. Cannot get too worked up about it.

8 o'clock. Scott taps on the door. Looks more tired than me.

8:15. Go downstairs to breakfast. Breakfast a worse mistake than dinner. Colon cancer returns.

8:30. Call the airport about our luggage. The bags have now been traced en route from Milan. Airport promises us they will have them for us by the time we are ready to leave for the ship.

4 o'clock. We are ready to leave for the ship. Luggage has not arrived.

4:30. Get to the dock. Have first glimpse of the ship. It is a beautiful sight.

5:30. Wish I were an equally beautiful sight. Scott and I board ship. I resemble a dirty dusting rag. People on the deck avoid me—cameras are purposefully focused away from my direction.

6 o'clock. The anchor is being lifted. There is a shout from dockside. An airport car pulls up. Our luggage has arrived.

6:15. I greet my suitcase as I never greeted Mitch in all our years of marriage. I hurry down to the cabin and unpack.

6:20. I make a discovery. All those dresses that I took out to iron just before leaving home—I forgot to re-pack them. I have not one dress. None. Nada. Glance briefly at nightgown, but no chance. Decide to crawl into bed and sob.

7 o'clock. Get settled in the cabin. It is the size of Molly's Barbie playhouse. Ceiling comes up to shoulder level. Practice trying to walk across room. Find that best results are achieved by slouching my back almost parallel to the floor and bending my knees in a deep plié, reminiscent of Quasimodo. Stagger to bunk and collapse in profound despair.

8 o'clock. Loud gong rings. Assume it's a call to man the lifeboats. Shoot to my feet and bash head on bulkhead. When vision clears, open door cautiously, spot purser, ask what's going on. Panic was unnecessary. It turns out to be the dinner bell. Get dressed in my madras shorts. They look mighty interesting, next to Scott's black-tie ensemble.

8:30. Cannot go through with it. Cannot face going into the dining room in a pair of madras shorts. Ended up having a tray sent to me in my cabin.

9 o'clock. Well, the day is finally over, and so is this morbid account. I am now settled in my snug bunk, dreamily looking through a magazine. All the dramas of the trip are behind us now, and before us lies nearly a week of eventless contentment and peace. You may not hear from me again until we land.

Raising My Titanic

Day 3

Or again, you may.

Last night, at two-seventeen in the morning, the ship hit a storm. This ship is not supposed to hit storms. I was up all night, expecting to be sunk at any moment. Tried to think of storms in their romantic context, like the one in *Brideshead Revisited*. This did not help. Especially as I spent most of the night in the bathroom, throwing up.

Fact: It is very hard to throw up into a moving toilet.

Lurched into Scott's cabin this morning, pleading for some Dramamine. (With touching faith in the magic of this trip, it had not even occurred to me to pack any.) Scott said he had something much better for seasickness, a little adhesive patch that you put behind your ear. With more touching faith, I put the little patch behind my ear. Approximately an hour passed. I did not notice any cessation of my seasickness—but I did notice a rather pronounced cessation of my vision.

When I complained of this to Scott, he read the warning on the box.

"Now that you mention it," he told me cheerfully, "it does say that the patch can cause blurriness of vision—and if that happens, you're supposed to discontinue use immediately."

Use discontinued immediately, but blurriness did not. Privately decided that the blurriness had not, in fact, been caused by the patch at all—it was the onset of a stroke.

Decided I'd better not take any medicine for awhile.

Spent most of my day alongside the toilet.

Aside from this entertainment, there was little else I could do. Being unable to see is not an ideal situation at any time, but it is especially undesirable when you have the Gottfried project to finish. Forget reading the fine print—I was having trouble keeping the cover of the files in focus.

Nothing to do but watch videos. All that was left in the library were horror movies, so my whole day was punctuated by screams and growls. Sounded a whole lot like me in the bathroom.

Weather unbelievable. Huge, endless waves, pitching and rolling. Ship in hourly danger of sinking.

Decided that I would rather meet Death face-to-face on the deck than be surprised in my cabin. So around four o'clock, I put on my warm cape, lurched up the stairs and spent an hour by the ship's railing.

The reason I spent an hour by the railing was not because I was enjoying myself but because I could not move. The moment I reached the deck, my cape, seized by the wind, started flapping high in the air like a giant bat. I clutched onto the rail, unable to let go, for fear the wind would parachute me and my cape right over the edge of the ship.

Finally I was rescued. One of the pursers came on the deck, saw my plight, and held my cape down. Now, out of embarrassment, I'll have to avoid him for the rest of the trip.

Raising My Titanic

Day 4

Cruise of Death continues. Last night the worst storm yet.

After breakfast, landed in Lake Gatoon. Scott went on to see the architectural treasures of the place, but I demurred. I told him my eyes were still too blurred to appreciate their beauties.

(These same eyes were, however, not too blurred to appreciate the beauties of a nearby jewelry stall, at which I haggled for and bought a hundred and sixty dollars' worth of sterling silver jewelry.)

Came back to the ship and found that God has punished me for this endearing and very human little hypocrisy. Scott, who knows about these things, said that I had been taken for a ride— that the jewelry isn't sterling at all.

Went back to my cabin and watched more horror films.

Emerged in time for dinner. I have been taking all meals in my cabin, ostensibly because of poor health, but really because of my lack of clothes. But tonight cabin fever hit with a vengeance. I had to get out of that tiny room, madras shorts and all. I asked Scott to come with me but he said he wasn't feeling too well and wanted to sleep.

No one in the dining room seemed to mind the shorts. As a matter of fact, I found myself seated at a table next to a charming man who didn't seem to mind anything at all about me. And, fuzzy as my vision is, I could still see with remarkable clarity that he's totally adorable, and wears no wedding ring.

Am feeling much more cheerful about this trip.

Day 5

Last night's storm was unbelievable. Felt very queasy this morning, but thought I'd better have breakfast. Suspect this desire had less to do with hunger than with hope that my new friend would be there in the dining room. Asked Scott to go with me, but he said he wasn't feeling up to it.

Sure enough, the man was at my table, and as friendly as ever. Another spirited little conversation ensued. This time I led it cagily into personal grounds, told him all about how hard it was being a single mother, and how difficult it was finding a decent man in Hollywood.

He put his hand on mine.

"Any man would be lucky to get you," he told me warmly. "If I were straight, I'd marry you myself."

Decided to skip lunch.

Later

Trip curtailed with unexpected abruptness.

Learned, when we reached the Panama Canal, that in our absence a 5.8 earthquake had hit Los Angeles. My only thought was to get back to Molly as soon as possible.

Scott was wonderful. Magnificent. Pulled every string imaginable. He hired a seaplane to take us back to Acapulco, and from there, got us on the next plane to Los Angeles.

Raising My Titanic

I told him to stay and enjoy the rest of the cruise but he said he'd rather be at home himself. He admitted he'd been feeling pretty terrible ever since the trip began. Didn't want to hear that.

Landed at LAX around midnight and took the shuttle bus to long-term parking. Realized, as we looked around the ocean of cars, that we had not paid any attention whatsoever to where we had parked.

Arrived home at dawn.

I wondered, as I walked into my sad and empty apartment, what actual good my dramatic return had done. Molly was still with Mitch, and she wouldn't be coming home to me any earlier—earthquake or no earthquake. Felt pretty foolish, especially as, ten minutes after I walked in the door, another earthquake hit.

All in all, I think dying during the storms at sea would have been more picturesque.

So here I am, back from my dream trip: legally blind, skinny as a pencil, totally untanned, frantic about Scott, and with nothing to show for my sumptuous vacation except a trunkful of fake jewelry and a working knowledge of every horror movie filmed in the last three decades.

June 28

Molly has returned. She looks different: stronger, taller. I was overjoyed to see her—covered her with kisses. She said she'd had a wonderful time, but gave no details. I said I'd had a wonderful time, too, but gave no details either. Which gives me hope that her time with Mitch was as rotten as my time on the cruise.

I had a little welcome-home present waiting for her: a dozen Archie comic books. I read two to her tonight, and she loved them. But then she said that she preferred Veronica to Betty—that Veronica was much prettier and funnier—and she hoped Archie would end up with her. I was aghast. I took up the cudgels on warm, sweet Betty's behalf and we fought about these stupid cartoon characters for nearly an hour.

It wasn't until after I put her to bed that the significance hit me. We all know who Veronica is. And in case you hadn't noticed, my name's Betty.

Later

Scott just called. He's got a fever of 102. I told him if it's not down by tomorrow I'm taking him to the hospital.

Raising My Titanic

June 29

It's okay. Fever's down. He's fine. He's fine.

June 30

Returned to the office today. Was very nervous about telling Peter that I hadn't been able to do any work on the trip. Came up with several excellent and unusual excuses. Was even prepared to return the Gucci luggage. But, to my joyous disbelief, discovered that the whole Gottfried deal had been called off the day after I left home. "I hope you didn't spend all your time on the project," Peter threw at me casually. I bit my lip, looked like the pietà, and said nothing.

For punishment, I gave him one of the fake silver key chains.

July 1

Cheryl's miniseries is finished. Her life is on hiatus, so she's taken over mine. Yesterday she came by, looked me over critically, and told me that I had aged terribly since she last saw me. She says it's my hair, that the gray has definitely gone into the danger zone, and that it's time to do something about it. Within minutes, she was on the phone, making an appointment for me to see a "hair genius" she knows. I heard her whisper to the receptionist at the beauty shop that it was an emergency.

And now I have returned home with new hair. Hair that's as taupe-colored as it was when I was in the first grade. Hair with not a speck of gray in it. It's amazing how guilty I feel—like I'm trying to pull a fast one on the world. I remind myself of the pathetic old man in *Death in Venice,* dyeing his hair and moustache black, in order to attract the beautiful boy, and then dropping dead in his beach chair.

On the other hand, I do look awfully good. Bought myself a cute tortoiseshell barrette. Goes well with all that taupe.

July 3

Tomorrow's the Fourth of July. God, I love that holiday. Went to the drugstore after work, and bought all sorts of wonderful things—tiny sparklers, striped bunting, an Uncle Sam mask. Even bought an ice cream cake, decorated to look like a flag, with little blueberries for the stars. This last purchase proved to be a mistake, however. There was horrific traffic on Coldwater and by the time I got home the cake had completely melted. Will have a patriotically colored backseat for years to come.

Raising My Titanic

But nothing spoils this mood of holiday nostalgia and reverie.

The Fourth of July brings back some of the most wonderful memories of my life.

Every year, when I was a little girl, my parents and I would drive down to Long Beach to visit Aunt Becky. For weeks before, I would look forward to the ritual. The hot, windy journey in Dad's Lincoln convertible. Exploring Aunt Becky's weird and wonderful house; bouncing on the trampoline; eating the figs off the fig tree; pretending to drive the cars rusting in the front yard.

I don't think I ever saw my mother so relaxed as she was on those hot July afternoons. In the presence of her older sister she seemed to become a carefree little girl again. The way she laughed, the way she let me do whatever I wanted, the way she lost the anxious line between her eyes. I think that's one reason I love my Aunt Becky so much—because she made Mama's face look young.

We'd have a huge lunch, and then afterwards we'd go to the park. The place was always packed; there'd be picnics, races, games, striped bunting, apple pies. Sometimes I wonder if I've embroidered upon the reality somewhat. But no, I think it all really happened just the way I remember.

Finally, at dusk, we'd all assemble on the bleachers. I'd be tired from the day, and lean my head on Mama's shoulder. Someone would make a speech. Some awful soprano would sing the national anthem. And then the fireworks would begin.

They were the best fireworks in the world. Bar none. Perfect fireworks blooming in the warm, night-scented air.

And we'd always play a special game around them. The first firework of the evening was always mine. The next belonged to Mama, the third was my Dad's, the fourth was Aunt Becky's. And then back to me again. It was maybe the most exciting concept of my childhood. That the next firework was going to be mine.

July 4

Made great plans for tonight. Decided that Molly's finally the right age to appreciate the Fourth of July. Called around and found a park in Pacific Palisades that's having a fireworks show at seven-thirty. Am so excited to think that my baby and I are forging a tradition of our own.

Later

At two o'clock, I went into Molly's room.

"Honey," I said, "we've got a big evening tonight, and I don't want you overtired. It's time to take a nap now."

"No," she told me.

I remembered the brilliant strategy I'd read about in the latest issue of *Parents* magazine.

"Let me give you a choice," I told her brightly. "If you take a nap, I will put on the Peter Rabbit tape. I will give you apple juice. We will go see fireworks tonight. You may wear your new red dress."

Raising My Titanic

I let this glory sink in and then added darkly, "And if you do *not* take a nap, there will be no Peter Rabbit tape. There will be no apple juice. There will be no red dress. There will be no fireworks. And all the angels in Heaven will weep." Impressively I paused. "Which do you choose?"

Molly hesitated for only a moment.
"Weeping angels," she said coolly.

July 5

Molly never took the nap, but of course we ended up seeing the fireworks anyway. She went crazy over them—loved them as much as I did. But she absolutely refused to play the fireworks game. She told me it was stupid, and she made up a game of her own, in which *all* the fireworks were hers.

July 6

Very ominous goings-on at work.
Peter had the flu this weekend, so he spent the whole time in bed, watching videos. This morning, he came back to work, risen like a phoenix from the ashes of Sudafed, called us all into his

office, and announced that Bookworm was now going into the video business.

No one at the office, especially Peter, knows anything about the video business. And of course this is precisely what has made the whole plan completely irresistible to him.

Last week he bought the rights to a little children's book called *The Strawberry Parfait.* Up until today, we were going to turn it into our usual book-on-tape; but Peter's now decided that this will be our test case, our prototype—our First Video.

He keeps telling us he's got everything under control, but there's a shrill fanatical tone to his voice that is getting me very nervous.

His first move was to find this video production company in São Paulo that does everything on the cheap. I've seen some of their faxes, and am very suspicious. I keep waiting for a phone call from the feds.

But I have one comfort. This video is one project I will *not* be involved in. Peter made that quite, unflatteringly clear this morning. He told me I'm to stick with the audio side of the business. There, he says, I'm competent—barely. But the new video line is his baby.

Raising My Titanic

July 7

Molly's birthday tomorrow. I can't believe she's going to be five. I went through all the photographs tonight. Her first birthday, with the little red-and-white-striped dress and her cake-covered hands. Her second birthday at the park, and that carousel horse she fell in love with. Her third birthday at the zoo, and her refusing to leave the koalas. Her fourth birthday with the clown and the balloon hat.

How terrifyingly true all the cliches are. That baby—that tiny girl—where is she now? Gone. Completely gone. Yes, I still have the red-and-white dress, and the balloon hat. But the dress would fit a doll; and the hat, lovingly put away in my hope chest, popped long ago. I adore that sassy little girl I live with. I have totally given my heart to her—but where's my baby?

July 8

Molly woke me up at six, full of birthday excitement. She can't believe she's five, either.

"I am now older than Jenny," she announced with awe. Jenny is the heroine in her favorite bedtime book. "I used to think I'd never be as old as Jenny and now she could be my little sister."

I think that scared us both a little.

After breakfast, I gave her her presents. The A.A. Milne books didn't go over too well, but the set of Little Birthday Ponies—each one with its birthday horn and party hat—was a big hit. But the best present was a beautiful doll called Amanda, dressed in a blue-and-white checked sundress.

"Isn't her outfit cute?" I asked Molly. "I'd love to have one exactly like it—wouldn't you?"

And then, when she said yes, I whipped out two more packages. One was for Molly, the other for me: blue-and-white sundresses that matched Amanda's.

It was a great moment. We named ourselves the "Checkered Sisters" and decided to form a singing group.

This is Mitch's year to have Molly for her birthday (I get even numbers, he gets odd), so at ten o'clock, I took her over there. He was waiting by the curb. When he saw Molly and Amanda and me getting out of the car, all in our matching dresses, he just leaned against the building and howled with laughter.

It's moments like that that make me realize that no matter how bad my life might ever become nothing could be worse than still being with Mitch.

Didn't feel up to much of anything today. Went to the mall for a little, but didn't find anything. Finally came home, sat on the floor of Molly's room, and had a birthday party with the little ponies.

Raising My Titanic

Mitch brought her back at nine. The Amanda dress was crumpled up at the bottom of her suitcase, and Molly was dressed in a jeans skirt, clogs, and a tank top. Her birthday gift from Veronica.

Later

Went to the post office today at lunch. Sent a big parcel to my cousin Peggy's little girl.

Molly spent much of the evening looking for her jeans skirt, clogs, and tank top.

July 11

Got an invitation this morning for my high school reunion. Reacted with shrill and gleeful scorn. Are they kidding? Me at a high school reunion? Tore the invitation to bits.

Later

Bought a new taupe silk blouse. That, and my new taupe hair, plus the latest batch of photographs of Molly has made me reconsider. Maybe going to the reunion wouldn't be such a bad idea. Maybe it would even be fun. Right. And maybe I am Queen of Romania.

Later

Have taped invitation back together. I'm going.

Later

Am starting to obsess on this reunion. I keep remembering a story my father once told me about a Hungarian friend of his called Laszlo. Laszlo grew up very poor in a little town near Budapest. All through his youth, he dreamed about leaving, coming to America, and finding fame and fortune. And the crowning point of the dream would be the day he returned to Hungary. He would drive along the main street of his old town in a chauffeur-driven limousine, and all the people from his childhood would gape and envy and admire.

Well, Laszlo did make it to Hollywood; and he did become a famous producer. And sure enough, one day he got a letter, inviting him back to his home town for an old friend's wedding. He flew back, and even went so far as to hire the limousine. But when he drove around the old neighborhood, and saw how shabby and sad it looked, he lost all interest in the dream. He had the chauffeur park the car a few blocks from the wedding, and he walked the distance.

I don't know why that story should come to mind. I really don't think that my appearance in my asthmatic Dodge Aspen is going to be too violent a blow to my ex-classmates' self-esteem. Still. I have those pictures of Molly to show—and that will be triumph enough.

Later

Still obsessing on this reunion. What will it be like to see everyone again, after all these years? Well, to be honest, I guess I don't mean *everyone*. What I guess I really mean is Judy Loeb.

Judy Loeb, my nemesis all through high school. The other straight-A student, the other star of the Tuesday Night Drama Group. We were rivals for everything. She got the lead in *The Glass Slipper*, but I got the tennis trophy. She made student body president, but I was editor of the literary magazine. And we tied for valedictorian.

It's amazing the pull that the past can have. And how those childhood rivalries can help shape your whole life. I wonder, now that I think about it, how many things I've done—or haven't done—simply because of Judy Loeb and wanting to be one up on her. And it's especially ironic because the day we graduated high school, I lost track of her entirely.

But I know one thing—that old rivalry still has its power. I spent all afternoon wondering what Judy's going to wear to the reunion and how I can look better.

A comforting thought: She can't be *too* famous, or I would surely have heard of her.

A horrible thought: Maybe she's become a best-selling writer, using a pseudonym. Wouldn't it be awful to get to the reunion and find out that Sidney Sheldon is really Judy Loeb?

Or maybe she's married to a doting husband and has four beautiful children. But I've beaten her there, no matter what. There's only one Molly, and she's *my* firework.

July 20

It's midnight but I can't even think about sleeping. I've got to tell someone about the reunion, and it's too late to call Scott.

The party was at nine, at the Marina Yacht Club. Decided to wear my yellow linen suit with the new silk blouse. Careery, but not aggressive; successful, without being showy.

Got lost on the drive. Asked directions. Got lost again. Arrived at the Yacht Club half an hour late. Got out of the car. Suit a disaster. One enormous wrinkle. I looked like a canary who had been put through a grater.

Feeling less than my best, I walked into the room. It was full of middle-aged strangers. God, what a shock. For a moment I had the poignant hope that I was in the wrong place. And then I happened to pass a swinging door with a beveled mirror on the top; and there I was, looking every bit as old as anyone there.

·　　·　　·

Raising My Titanic

Things perked up for me a little after my first drink. A few of the faces began to come into clearer focus, and in them I recognized traces of girls I had once known, about sixty million years ago.

There was Carol Walsh—the former star of our ballet class. Now two hundred pounds and a trucker.

There was Ivy Rupine—little Miss Goody Goody. Now sporting pink and green hair and a ring through her nose.

Things were definitely getting interesting.

After a second drink, I started talking to these strangers. These women that I had once played volleyball with, agonized over math quizzes with, traded lunches with. Funny how little mannerisms, tricks of the voice, expressions come back to you. Like the way Maggie Kennerly says "Awww...." How could I have forgotten that? It was part of my life for so many years.

What I saw was fascinating, quite a statement on the American woman. Half the class had turned into big-time career women: journalists or lawyers or in the unbelievable case of Tanya Silverman, a doctor. (Listen, I was her partner in junior biology, and I'll never forget what she did to that frog.) And the other half were pure, simple, 1950s housewives.

Showed off Molly's pictures to everyone I could grab.

After my third drink Judy Loeb walked in.

I turned and there she was. It all happened so fast that I didn't have time to erect my critical defenses. And so the awful truth took me like the Greeks took the Trojans.

Judy Loeb looked absolutely gorgeous.

Still slim, but with a gentle rippling effect that I don't remember her having in high school.

Still blonde, but with a wheatier ripeness in her hair.

Still the same damned perfect skin.

She was dressed in a cute little green culotte outfit and bolero jacket. Whimsical without being over the top. An absolutely inspired choice for a high school reunion at a yacht club. How could I have been so stupid as to come dressed as an insipid giant yellow wrinkle?

I just kept staring at her, telling myself wanly that none of this mattered. I mean, just because Judy Loeb looked a hundred times better than I did didn't mean a thing. After all, she could still be utterly miserable inside.

I went up to her. We hugged and squealed, did all those reunion things.

Then I pulled away.

"So, Judy," I asked, trying to sound casual, "how's your life been going?"

"Fantastic," she said.

Nuts.

I asked what line of work she was in, and barely kept myself from shouting out, "You don't have to tell me—I know. You're Sidney Sheldon!"

But what she actually said was, "I give facials in a little town in Oregon."

Raising My Titanic

I stared at her. Judy Loeb was giving facials in a little town in Oregon? *Judy Loeb?* It was completely unbelievable.

She saw my look and she laughed.

"Not what you expected?"

"Oh, I think it's great," I told her. "Los Angeles is getting crazier and crazier. I'm sure where you are is paradise."

She nodded emphatically. I plowed on, needing to know all.

"And what about family? Do you have a husband?"

She laughed.

"Does my lesbian lover count?"

Again I just stared. I cannot tell you what all this was doing to me inside. It was like one of those cartoons where the little gopher runs amok and completely tears up the field. I mean, my God. For years I had been living under the shadow of Judy Loeb. Feeling her breathing down my neck—feeling that wherever she was, she was doing exactly the same thing I was doing, only better. And it had all turned out to be shadowboxing.

I felt tears coming into my eyes. I sniffed hideously to keep my nose from running. Then I started to laugh. And then she started to laugh. And all at once I felt this amazing weight drop from me. I realized that I actually liked Judy Loeb. That she and I could be friends, and that maybe we could have been friends right from the beginning.

She asked what I had been doing with my life and I told her. I told her all about my job and my hopes for a Spoken Word Grammy and about Molly. And here's the really interesting part—Judy didn't seem any more jealous of my life than I was of hers.

A humbling and fascinating thought. Could this possibly mean that there is actually room for *both* of us in this world?

Then Judy and I began reminiscing about the old days, especially those Tuesday nights with the Drama Group. She brought up names I hadn't thought of in years. Dennis Michaels. Troy Ryerson. She told me she had kept up with a lot of the old gang.

I found my heart was suddenly suffocating me.

"And Buddy Villiers?" I asked. "Have you heard anything from him?"

She shook her head.

"Not for a while. I know he married and moved to Florida after college. The last I heard, he was in Tallahassee working for a television station. But that was quite a while ago."

It was strange, so strange—hearing Buddy being talked about after all these years. And even stranger to think of him still in the world: living somewhere, doing something—right now, at this moment.

Finally, Judy and I ran out of things to say to each other. I asked her for one of her business cards in case I was ever in Oregon and needed a facial. The card had a drop of oil spilled in the corner.

And then I left the reunion. There was no reason to stay any longer.

Raising My Titanic

3:00 A.M.

Feel very grumpy, wildly restless. I just went through the closet and dragged out old boxes full of memorabilia. I sorted through them all. My high school yearbook. Faded inscriptions. Class notes for long-forgotten tests. I feel so sad. Flooded by the sense of time going so fast—and of so much waste.

Finally, I came upon a letter from Buddy.

For a moment, I couldn't place it. And then I remembered. It had accompanied a book he had once given me, a collection of e. e. cummings fairy tales, with the picture of an elephant on the cover.

I recognized his handwriting right away.

> Dear Betty,
> They wrapped the book before I could write this inscription, so through the aid of a paper clip you can use this little note.
>
> As I see it, this book and I have much in common. For one thing, we are both yours. For another, you can't give either of us back. You have probably seen us both before, but if you look a little more closely, you will find many hidden surprises.
>
> You cannot lose either of us, for we both have a habit of cropping up unexpectedly. The book and I are both one of many, and that is as it should be; but unlike the book, I fully intend to remain your

favorite. The book is called "The Little Elephant." I, too, am short and won't forget you. The book and I need you, for without you to hold us, we are useless.

Both of us will remain the same down through the years, remembering, needing, unreturnable. And neither of us will ever let you go. And at least, we won't let you go too far.

Buddy.

I started crying like a lunatic.
I think I'll have a drink.

4:00 A.M.

Just dialed Tallahassee information and asked for Buddy Villiers's telephone number. The operator told me there was no one listed by that name.

Just had another drink and this one's put me over the edge. I'd better go to bed.

July 24

Mitch has gotten married.

I keep staring at this sentence. I read it over and over, but I can't get it to mean anything. Mitch has gotten married—and he isn't married to me. For so long, all I wanted was for Mitch to be married to me. And then he was. And then he wasn't. And now he is married to someone else.

I had no clue that this was going to happen. He called me at work yesterday, asking if Molly could spend the night. I said sure, and brought her over. This morning I heard a little tap at the door—usually Mitch brings Molly up in the elevator but today she was alone. Excited, jumping up and down, cheeks hot pink with importance as she told me the big news.

I tried not to show her how hard this big news hit me. I alternated between acting very cool one minute and scavenging shamelessly for details the next. Molly happily supplied the information. Apparently, it had all been a big surprise to her. The ceremony was performed by a justice of the peace. Mitch wore a blue suit (the Armani that I bought him?) and Veronica wore a lace minidress. Never, Molly told me solemnly, had there been a lovelier bride. The service was short, with Molly the only wedding guest. Well, Mitch was always one for understatement.

Then they came home and drank champagne, and both Veronica and Molly woke up with hangovers. Molly treasures this new bond between them. How wonderful.

Later

I am finding it very hard to cope with this news. Perhaps a list will help sort things out.

MARY SHELDON

VARIOUS REACTIONS ON HEARING THAT MY EX-HUSBAND HAS REMARRIED

1. His life is wonderful, mine is awful. He has found someone, I haven't. He will be happy forever, I will be miserable. Molly will go live with him and his new wife, and I will be homeless on the streets.

2. . . . .

So much for the list.

Later

A lady in my building told me about this wonderful psychologist she knows.

Have decided to seek refuge in the arms of therapy.

July 25

Today was my first appointment with Dr. Hoag. Walked over to his office during my lunch hour. My God, these guys have nice waiting rooms. Felt incredibly nervous. Was so afraid that someone I knew would see me going in—and report it to Peter or, worse, Mitch. Was even more afraid the doctor would take one look at me, have the doors double-bolted, and the next thing I knew I'd be in the psychiatric wing of Cedars.

Raising My Titanic

But Dr. Hoag turned out to be a very mellow fellow. He put me in a nice easy chair and told me to say anything that was on my mind. I told him about the divorce, and Mitch's remarrying. I tried to sound very coherent and sane, and I made sure I had plenty of eye contact with him. (I read somewhere that mass murderers never give eye contact.)

Then he started asking about what my marriage had been like, and my childhood. To my horror, I found myself in sudden floods of tears, and girded myself anew for the psychiatric wing. But Dr. Hoag kept listening, without saying a word. Then, when I finished, he shook his head and said that with the incredible amount of loss and pain I'd had in my life it was a miracle I'd survived at all.

He ended the hour by saying I must be a very strong and wonderful person.

It's not often I've been called strong and wonderful by someone with a PhD. I paid my hundred-and-twenty-five dollars with a seraphic smile on my face and decided to make a second appointment for next week. I like therapy a lot.

Later

Well, not much time to gloat over my personal worth. Disaster at work. The finished *Strawberry Parfait* video arrived back from São Paulo, and it's terrible. Completely unusable. So bad that I'm not even tempted to tell Peter "I told you so."

Peter is frenzied—I've never seen him so hysterical. As I write this, I can hear things being thrown around his office. I'm not even sure his crystal Boda zoo has survived.

Half an Hour Later

Peter finally emerged from his office. Calm and smiling. He called us all in to say that he has a new plan. The São Paulo video is to be scrapped, and the company sued for every cruzeiro they have. But we are by no means giving up on the project.

A new video is to be made. Another artist will be found, who will immediately create three hundred charming new pictures. A new videographer will also be discovered—a talented professional who can shoot stop-action animation with tender, sensitive skill. The fact that Peter intends to pay these people even less than their São Paulovian counterparts does not worry him in the least. Nor does the fact that he has promised the finished video to stores by the end of the year.

As Peter was leaving the room, he turned back to deliver one final casual line. Unfortunately, due to his busy schedule, he is no longer able to mastermind the project. In fact, he's too busy to do anything on it at all.

So he's given it to me.

Raising My Titanic

July 26

Dr. Hoag called this morning. It seems he's written a textbook about schizophrenia, and was wondering if, with all my show-business connections, I could get it done as a book-on-tape. Preferably to be read by Dusty Hearkness.

Said I would try. Then I canceled my next appointment.

So much for therapy.

July 30

I went into the Hamburger Hamlet for lunch today and there, sitting together on one side of a booth, were Mitch and Veronica.

So I have seen her at last. Mitch's new wife. She's even younger and blonder, more beautiful and bosomy than I had imagined. She had her hand on Mitch's shoulder—just where I used to put my hand.

I wanted to go up to them, casual, smiling, and congratulate them on their marriage. I envisioned the scene. I rehearsed it. But I just couldn't do it.

As I was hurrying out of the restaurant, I saw Mitch wave to the waitress for the check. On his hand was a big wedding ring.

He wouldn't wear a wedding ring when he was married to me.

August 5

I hate this video. I hate this video more than I have ever hated anything in my life.

I have spent the last four days trying to find an artist and a videographer. Have come up with zero. The talented ones are too busy, and the untalented ones are too eager—at least, until they hear the price we're offering. Then they usually slam down the phone.

August 8

Huge relief. Have finally found a young artist named Karen Axelrod. She and her husband have a new baby, and she'd love to earn a little extra money. (Emphasis on the *little*.) I told her how important it was to have the pictures done on schedule, and she said that wouldn't be a problem. Her husband stays at home, and looks after their little boy, and she has promised me that she can paint very fast. So I hired her.

And as far as the videographer goes, I have found a young man called Giles down in Burbank who assured me that he'll be the perfect man for the job—once he finds out how to film stop-action animation. But by this point, I was so desperate, I hired him, too.

Raising My Titanic

August 9

Got a call from Karen. Her husband has left her. She says she's still eager to do the project—but would Peter mind if the pictures were delivered around Christmas? At my hysterical laughter, she hung up the phone.

August 10

To my admiration and shock, Federal Express delivered a batch of paintings from Karen this morning. They are radiant. They are wonderful. They are on time.

Had them messengered to Giles. He called me up to thank me and mentioned that he had still not figured out how to do stop-action animation. So I canceled all my meetings, drove to Burbank, and spent the day working with him on the video.

Basically, what you do is this: You prop up the picture you want to film, and you film it. Then you go on to the next picture.

We worked for nine hours today, but it was worth the time. I feel that great progress has been made.

Next Day

Giles called. Said he just finished editing all the work we did yesterday. It came to thirty-five seconds' worth of screen time. Since the video is going to be an hour long, and due in the stores in less than three months' time, it does not take a math genius to figure out that we are in major trouble.

Have canceled all appointments for the next month.

Sometime

Working, working. Karen sends fresh batches of pictures daily; Giles and I shoot them. Hour after hour after hour. Locating the right picture. Synchronizing the text with the shot. Deciding on the camerawork. Doing the camerawork. Redoing the camerawork. Can only hope this video wins a Library Notable Award. Better yet, the Pulitzer. That would make the whole thing worthwhile.

No, on second thought, I don't think it would.

August 30

My life is over, I am wrinkled and gray, and the last time I saw her Molly had gone for a Ph.D. But the video is finished. Giles— he uses a walker now—is sending me the final cut tonight.

Raising My Titanic

August 31

The cut arrived. Molly and I, in great excitement, made popcorn, cuddled on the sofa, and turned on the VCR to watch the masterpiece.

Within two minutes, flop sweat was pouring out of my palms.

The video is terrible. Completely unacceptable. Worse than the one from São Paulo. It cannot go out on the market like this. Bookworm would be the laughingstock of the industry. I have to call Karen and ask her to paint forty-seven more pictures by tomorrow. And I have to call Giles and tell him that I counted one hundred and twenty-three mistakes in the filming. (Molly says there were two hundred and thirteen but then she's impossibly perfectionistic.)

I want to die. I want to go back to the Panama Canal and be wrecked in a giant storm.

September 2

Molly and I went to the park yesterday. Again we tried taking the training wheels off her bicycle. Again it didn't work. What's wrong with me, that I can't teach my little girl to ride a bicycle? Feel incredibly defensive and inadequate and hostile.

Tried to make up for my bad mothering. Came home and

showed Molly how to set a table, read her a few scenes of *As You Like It,* and taught her a little French song. A touch of overkill, perhaps? Molly finally begged me just to let her go in the den and watch television.

> cjdkeitughtjrkekfjkl;jkl;jkl;disml'alblkdjkejdnvkl;el
> fisjdkslslslslslslkjfgjkefaioaekicvnkvdnmdvjkdfo;fei
> oeruifbjkdfjkyrljlj!!!!!!!!!!!!!!!!!!!!!!!

Came in to find this typed onto my computer. Molly wrote it. She says it's in Chinese, that it's about mothers, and that it's too rude to translate.

September 3

Labor Day. Peter fired the whole office on Friday because we didn't want to work today. Then realizing what that meant— that he would have to man the entire place himself—he changed his mind, rehired us, and went to Catalina.

I took Molly to Disneyland. Didn't tell her in advance where we were going—only said that we were spending the day with some friends. Right before we reached the park, I told her to close her eyes until I'd counted to ten. Then, at the count of ten, she opened her eyes. And there was Disneyland. Her little face at

Raising My Titanic

that moment was one of the pictures I'm going to carry with me until I die.

But, "I knew we were going here all along," she assured me coolly. "I was just looking surprised so you'd be pleased."

We had a fantastic day. Went on just about every ride. We could never agree on which one to go on next. I like the gentle rides, like Alice in Wonderland, Molly of course prefers the death-defying ones like Space Mountain. So we were democratic and took turns. (Molly did not particularly like this method but, as I continually reminded her, I was the one paying.)

Her favorite ride was Snow White's Scary Adventures. I had balked at taking her on this, because I remember how it had terrified me as a child. But she insisted. Well, it still terrified me—at one point during the ride, the part where the witch is about to hand Snow White the apple, I closed my eyes and told Molly to let me know when it was safe to look again.

"It's all over now Mama," she told me sweetly.

So I opened my eyes—just in time to see the witch hand Snow White the apple. I don't know who cackled more loudly, the witch or my daughter.

Molly adored seeing all the Disney characters walking around and managed to get in long analytic discussions with all those she encountered.

"Now, Fox, don't you agree that it was very cruel of you to trick Pinocchio out of his five golden pieces? I think this behavior is something you'll have to work on."

1 7 5

But the best moment of the day was what happened in the Tinkerbell Toy Shop. I gave Molly some money, and she spent nearly half an hour trying to decide what to buy. Next to the cash register were some little Dumbo erasers that I said reminded me of ones I had loved as a child. I pointed these out hopefully, but Molly wasn't interested in any Dumbo erasers.

Finally she made her choice—a stuffed Goofy doll—and I started to take it up to the cash register. But Molly said firmly that she wanted to pay for it herself. She led me to a far-off corner of the store, and told me to keep busy looking at the books. A few minutes later, she returned to me, bag in hand, her face pink with excitement.

As we left the store, she said, "I bet you wish you had bought one of those Dumbo erasers for yourself."

I said, "You know something, you're right."

And then, trembling with excitement, she reached into her bag, pulled out the eraser she had secretly bought, and handed it to me.

9:00 P.M.

Home now. Molly is asleep in her room. I'm in the living room, drinking wine, and just about to burst into tears.

It's no mystery why. The thing that I've been trying to push back for the last few weeks is coming up; even Disneyland couldn't

Raising My Titanic

quite fade it. Molly starts school tomorrow. Not day care, not preschool—real school. Real away-from-Mama, starting life in the big world school. I can't believe the moment has finally come.

I go into the closet and check her clothes. Tiny prim dress and sweater, heartbreakingly small oxfords.

It's as if I can actually see the shadows of the prison closing around my baby. It makes me want to scream, thinking that this will be the first of so many uniforms that Molly will have to wear throughout her life. In twenty years, what will it be? The neat suit and ruffled blouse of the successful working woman? My Molly— a successful working woman? Oh God, it turns the stomach.

Well, maybe she'll be one of the lucky ones and manage to escape the system. Be forever young and a free spirit forever. (When I drink wine, my radical proclivities tend to take over.)

I think it's the little oxfords that get to me the most. I remember buying Molly her first pair of shoes, those soft white satin shoes, in a size 000. The saleslady smiled at me when I bought them and said something about "how quickly they grow." But I didn't believe her—not really. I guess I thought Molly would be wearing size 000 shoes forever.

I just went into her room and checked on her. She was lying across the bed as only Molly can lie—sideways, diagonal and spider-like all at once. Her new Disneyland T-shirt was twisted around her middle. When I tried to straighten it, she sighed impatiently in her sleep. I left it that way. And her new Goofy was snuggled in her arms. It was comforting to see him there, with his wise, silly face.

Next Day

Took Molly in to school. She was very cool about the whole thing—and especially excited about wearing the new oxfords. She was a little uneasy, however, about my own appearance and made several suggestions on how it could be improved. Ultimately found myself wearing my best silk suit and more makeup than I would wear to a black-tie dinner party.

Her teacher, Mrs. Klein, seems cheerful and kind. Was relieved to find she's not too pretty. I don't need any more competition for Molly's affections. The classroom reminded me poignantly of my own first-grade room, and the play yard doesn't seem particularly lethal. Was tempted to recite to Mrs. Klein a long list of all Molly's little habits, but resisted the temptation. When I was a child we always felt so sorry for the kids whose parents did that.

Summoning all the heroism I had within me, I kissed Molly goodbye as casually as I could. As it turned out, the heroism was wasted. Halfway through the kiss, she was off to the toy corner.

Cried all the way to work. When I arrived, Peter called everyone into his office to look at me.

"This is what a mother looks like," he said soberly. "I hope this will prevent any of you who are thinking about having children from doing so."

Raising My Titanic

5:00 P.M.

Rushed home from work, filled with dread that after one day of school, Molly would have changed irredeemably. Was thrilled to find her in her usual seat in the den, wearing her usual T-shirt, putting on her usual Barbie Beauty Pageant, and eating her usual family-size bag of Doritos.

"How was school?" I choked.

She considered. "I don't remember too well, but I think it was okay."

Then she went back to Barbie.

I feel very encouraged. They may force her feet into oxfords, but they'll never get too far with her mind.

September 6

The video has won. I am dying daily. I have seven different types of cancer this week. Had planned to spend this evening editing, but I'm not going to. When the days dwindle down to a precious few, as they are rapidly doing in my case, it's time to reevaluate ones priorities.

September 8

The cavalry has come. The rescue squad has arrived.

My crazy Aunt Becky just called, full of excitement. She's bought this wonderful new camper, she's discovered this marvelous campsite in the woods above Seattle, and she wants Molly and me to fly up there this weekend and go camping with her. She went on and on and on about how we'd absolutely love it. All the comforts of home. Nature walks for Molly. Healthy air to combat the poisonous fumes of Los Angeles.

Without a single thought for my overcharged credit cards, my fear of flying, or the fact that the video still needs about ten thousand hours of work, I said yes immediately. I called the travel agent, made the reservations, and we leave on Saturday morning.

All seven types of cancer seem to be improving.

September 10

Went to the bookstore today, and picked up some books about Seattle. I'm getting terribly excited about the trip. The caffe latte bars sound wonderful, and apparently there's a great old marketplace where the fishmongers put on a show by throwing enormous fish back and forth. And I hear the Science Museum's out

Raising My Titanic

of this world—not to mention the aquarium and the antique stores. This trip will be a real cultural tour de force.

Had hoped to buy some warm camping clothes, but there's been no time. Anyway, Aunt Becky said that the weather's been beautiful up in Seattle, and my California things will do fine. And she specifically repeated that this campsite we're going to has "all the comforts of home." I guess that means it's near a mall—maybe even a mall with a caffe latte bar.

September 13

Well, I am home. Barely. Barely alive after the most hair-raising weekend of my life.

It all started out so happily, so innocently. After a very smooth flight Saturday morning, we arrived in Seattle around eleven. Aunt Becky greeted us, in her new camper. It's hard to believe this now, but when I first laid eyes on the thing, I thought it was cute. And it actually crossed my mind that one day it might be fun to get one just like it.

I had assumed that the camping portion of our trip would start that evening, and that we would spend the day exploring the cultural high spots of Seattle. But I was wrong. It seems that this particular campsite, so beloved of Aunt Becky, was many hours away, and that unless we started at once, we'd never make it.

We got into the camper. Molly, who is extremely possessive of Aunt Becky, wanted to sit beside her in the front seat. I was hoping that Aunt Becky would refer to the time-honored "children belong in the backseat" rule but either she hadn't heard of the rule, or she found Molly's company preferable to mine.

In any event, the two of them were soon cheerfully ensconced in the front seats, while I was in the backseat, many, many yards behind. At first, I tried to take part in the conversation, but the distance between us was so great, and it was so hard to shout over the camper engine, that I gave up entirely. Which resulted in my sitting in a somewhat sulky silence for the entire six-hour ride.

The sulkiness was due in part to the fact that I had not yet had my morning coffee. I had been saving myself for the caffe latte.

As we drove endlessly along, I noticed two things that I did not like. One was that the weather had turned even sulkier than I had, and two was that the farther we drove, the sparser and sparser the malls seemed to be getting.

Finally, just at twilight, we pulled into Aunt Becky's campsite.

How to describe this campsite? The word "damp" immediately comes to mind. So does "slimy." And "dark" and "depressing." But "freezing cold" is definitely the most accurate.

"Don't worry about a thing!" Aunt Becky said heartily. "I'll have the heater going in a jiffy."

Well, about thirty jiffies later, she gave up, admitting that she

Raising My Titanic

hadn't paid too much attention to what the camper salesman had told her about how the heater worked.

"That's all right," I said, with great bravura. "A little dinner will warm us up."

Proudly, Aunt Becky showed us her refrigerator. In it was cold milk and a box of Sugar Pops—the one cereal in the world I cannot stand. I told Aunt Becky that for some strange reason, I was suddenly not very hungry.

Molly, however, was in heaven. After saying balefully, "Mama never lets me have Sugar Pops. Mama never lets me have anything good," she finished off two bowls and said it was the best dinner she'd ever eaten.

The evening meal over, Aunt Becky decided that it was now time for our nature walk. I wasn't feeling terribly in the mood for the beauties of the wild, so I said I'd stay in the camper and work on ideas for the video.

No one tried to talk me out of my decision.

It was then five-thirty. Aunt Becky promised that she and Molly would be back in half an hour. Had to be back then, she explained with a light laugh. She hadn't wanted to mention it before, but there were bears around this particular campsite.

The two of them left, happily swinging clasped hands. I began my work. When I finished my work, it was six-thirty. No Aunt Becky and Molly. I tried to read. I read till seven. I tried to play solitaire. I played till seven-thirty. Finally, at seven-forty-five, I was at the point of getting out of the camper, charging into the bear-infested woods and hunting out my kin, when they returned—laughing, singing, swinging their clasped hands.

"That was the best time I've ever had!" Molly informed me. "Much better than Disneyland." Then she added darkly, "Mama never lets me take nature walks. Mama never lets me have any fun. And Mama especially never lets me bring home specimens."

"What do you mean—specimens?" I asked faintly.

She held out her hand. In it was the perfectly preserved skeleton of a frog.

After a grand scene in which I fully lived up to my ogre reputation, we all decided it was time to go to bed.

Getting the camper ready for the night was a challenging experience. First, the whole roof had to be unlatched, lifted four feet, and clicked into place. The camper now had a top that looked like a soufflé, and was just about as durable. I figured it would take a bear less than a minute to claw his way through it. Then Aunt Becky miraculously unfolded a bed from what used to be the roof, saying that she and Molly would sleep there. And my bed was the old familiar car seat, opened out, that I'd spent the whole day sitting on.

And there we were. No Eskimo in his igloo *sans* furs could have been more comfortable.

·   ·   ·

Raising My Titanic

I kept up the relentless bravado. I told myself that I would feel better after washing my face and brushing my teeth. Maybe the campsite even provided a place where nice, hot baths could be taken. I gathered up my chic Neiman Marcus toilette bag and fluffy Martex towel.

"Where are the bathrooms?" I asked.

Aunt Becky led Molly and me from the camper. We walked down a God-forsaken path in total darkness—Aunt Becky thinks that flashlights are for sissies. Finally, after three wrong turnings, and what, I swear, was the sound of moving bears, we found the bathroom. It looked just like the bathrooms my Texan grandmother used to describe to me—with the half moon on the door and the Sears Roebuck catalog used in place of toilet paper.

But, alas, I never got to fully make the comparison. Because these bathrooms were locked.

"How strange!" Aunt Becky said. "They were open the last time I was here! Well, I guess we'll just have to go in the woods."

I was not going in any woods.

Aunt Becky and Molly had a hilarious time, doing what they had to do, and then we trooped back to our home for the night.

In the twenty minutes we had been gone the temperature in the camper had dropped about fifteen degrees.

As icy wind poured into the canvas, I realized that Aunt Becky had been wrong. No, my delicate little Eileen West nightie that she had so blithely assured me would be fine, was not fine. It all but turned to ice on my body.

With a flourish, Aunt Becky pulled out some sleeping bags. She and Molly got the nice old-fashioned kind. But for me there was a special brand—something known as a "mummy" sleeping blanket. I know why it is called that. Because one night in this thing, and you wake up looking like the 300-year-old crone in *Lost Horizon*.

Aunt Becky and Molly hoisted themselves onto their bunk. It began to creak very ominously. I tried not to think of what the chances were of its crashing down upon me in the night—nor of my chances of surviving the crash. Then, for hours, the two of them talked and giggled above.

I lay on my back, mummified. No one had thought to bring a pillow, so I crumpled up the jacket of my best Liz Claiborne suit into a ball, and used that. The cold wind blew. The bears breathed. And then I turned my head and heard a very strange snapping noise. It was my hair, frozen to the pillow.

I did not get much sleep.

At around two in the morning, I started to get hungry. At three in the morning, I was hungrier than I had ever been in my life. I thought of the milk I had spurned at dinnertime and, cautiously, I felt my way over to the refrigerator. I found the handle, and gave a gentle pull. And that was when I realized. By opening out my seat into a bed, I had blocked the entrance to the refrigerator. There was no way I could get at it. Soon, the truth expanded

Raising My Titanic

itself into an even grimmer realization. My only choice was the Sugar Pops.

I feel about Sugar Pops the way I feel about cannibalism, but as those sheepish survivors always say, "I had no choice."

The Sugar Pops eaten, I tried once again to get to sleep. But my body was saving one last little trick: I suddenly realized I had to go to the bathroom. I really, really had to go to the bathroom.

I looked hopefully around for some sort of chamber pot—at this point, I would even have sacrificed my Neiman Marcus toilette bag. But I couldn't find anything. And the thought of going in my Mummy suit, of being locked in with it all night, was not to be considered for a moment.

It was the woods or nothing.

Cautiously, I slid open the door of the camper. This was not a terribly silent operation, but I didn't awaken Molly or Aunt Becky. This annoyed me more than slightly.

I crept out into the night, my nightgown crackling frozenly around my ankles. I found a little hill and did the deed. In doing so, I learned a very important lesson. Never do the deed on a hill.

With a very damp hem on my nightgown, I crept back to the camper.

And at around five in the morning, I finally managed to fall asleep.

"Rise and shine!" chirped Aunt Becky at five-fifteen.

• • •

I don't remember much of Sunday. Vague recollections come to mind of some very strident birdsong. Then Sugar Pops for breakfast. Then driving in the rain, six hours back to the airport. Then a very bumpy flight back to Los Angeles.

And here I am at last, back in my apartment. I feel better now. I have visited a mall. I have bought a new nightgown. I have washed my hair. I have eaten at a restaurant with silverware and French items on the menu.

The ordeal is over.

Later

Maybe not. A few minutes ago, I put Molly to bed. She gave me a big hug, then looked at me with a blissful expression on her face. "Mama, when can we buy a camper of our own?"

Wickedly, I suggested, "Why don't you ask your Daddy?"

Thoughts of Veronica encountering a bear flitted behind my angelic smile.

Raising My Titanic

September 15

Scott is in the hospital. He tells me it's not serious—just tests. But I'm pretty anxious.

I went to visit him. He was so up, so cute, flirting with all the nurses, making everyone feel happy.

September 16

Scott out of the hospital.

Later

Have been working solidly on the video. It's not going particularly well, but I'm not really caring. The image of Scott in that hospital bed.

The new receptionist at work has invited me to a party at her apartment tonight. Maybe I'll chuck the damn video and go.

September 17

Glad I went. Believe it or not, I met kind of an interesting guy.

His name is Edward Solley. He reminds me of a medieval Spanish knight—very tall and dark and graceful, with a courtly other-worldliness about him. And the most intriguing thing of all, he's a surfer.

He told me that, though he hasn't been doing it as much lately, he's one of the best surfers in all of Malibu. When he was in his twenties, he was called King of the Beach, and everyone was in awe of him.

How romantic. All kinds of appealing images come to mind. Days spent on golden sand, living the Zen life, shooting the curl. How eloquently and seductively Edward talks about it all. And boy, I bet he still looks good in Speedos.

Very subtly, I managed to give him my phone number. We were talking about books, and I wrote down a list of historical novels I thought he might enjoy reading. Wrote it down on the back of one of my bank deposit slips. Let's see if he takes the bait.

September 18

Bait has been taken. Edward called this morning. When I marveled that he had tracked me down, even though my number

Raising My Titanic

was unlisted, his pride in telling me that he'd gotten it from my bank deposit slip was adorable.

And he asked me out to dinner tonight. Oh, video, where is thy sting?

Later

Molly came home from school today, announcing proudly that she had learned to play jacks. I was enchanted. When I was a kid, jacks was my absolute speciality. I could beat everyone in school, except, of course, Diana Sherman. I got all nostalgic and excited, and promised Molly I'd give her a few pointers.

We drove by a toy store and I bought her her own set of jacks. Then we came home and started to play. Molly beat me. Played another game. Molly beat me again. I challenged her to a third game, but she gave me some spurious story about having to do her homework. Wouldn't let her get away with this. Made her play two more games. Finally beat her. Felt very ashamed of myself. Will tell this story to no one.

One awesome thought, though. I do believe Molly could even have beaten Diana Sherman.

September 19

First date with Edward. He picked me up from work at six. I met him in the lobby, so that Peter wouldn't get the chance to destroy the relationship before it began, and then he took me to a health-food restaurant. God, I hate health-food restaurants. Had to eat two doughnuts when I got home, to take the taste away.

But in spite of it all, it was a pleasant evening. It's very peaceful being with Edward. He's gentle, and soft-spoken and interested in all the right things. Meditation, higher consciousness, me.

And there's such a poignancy about him.

He told me a little about his history last night. He's the only son of parents who are in their late seventies. They're in the garment business, and all through his life, Edward has hated, passionately hated, the garment business. Yet he was constantly told that it was his destiny to take over after his father retires—and that if he didn't, he would fail at anything else he tried to do.

It's horrendous, the way his parents have systematically managed to wreck his life. Four months before Edward was supposed to graduate college, his mother broke her leg, and he had to drop out of school and help her. Must have been some fracture. One thing led to another, and he never got his degree.

Then later, he went into the Southwest furniture business. He was living in Santa Fe, making a fortune, almost had enough money to buy a condo—when his father had a heart attack and Edward was summoned home.

Raising My Titanic

Then, after that, he went down to Mexico as a silver exporter. Again, he was doing terrifically—better than any other salesman there—when his mother got emphysema. And back he had to come.

What's most touching is that all through this ordeal, Edward has never given up on a dream of his own. He wants to be a filmmaker, and to make an important independent film, something along the lines of Tarkovsky and Kurosawa.

To try and raise money for this film, he's been in all kinds of bizarre get-rich-quick businesses, like import-export and telemarketing and commodities brokering. But his luck has been awful. Twice, he's been cheated by partners just as a deal was about to get off the ground, and three times, the moment he got into the stock market, the economy bottomed out. So, at the moment, he's unemployed.

And when I asked him about his romantic past, he told me that that part of his life hadn't turned out any better—that, though he has always longed for a steady relationship, he's never once found a woman worthy to commit to.

And then he looked me straight in the eyes and said in a low voice, "But that could be changing."

I didn't know how to respond. After all I've gone through this year, I guess I've gotten pretty cynical. But inside, I must confess, I felt my heart do the old hopeful broad jump through my chest. Well, we shall see.

September 26

Have gone on a few more dates with Edward, and am still intrigued.

I've never met anyone like him. He's almost archetypal—it's as if all the good that was in the '60s has been personified in this one man. That sense of freedom, pure spirit, unattachment to worldly things. It's very bracing to be with him—when I am, I feel quite ashamed of my own temporal, mammon-related concerns.

And I'm so drawn to the idea of his being a surfer. It's endlessly fascinating, hearing him talk about it. What it's like to ride a tube wave, the way the jellyfish look in Maui, and all the odd old characters who used to hang around the beaches. I love it— it's like a magical mythology.

Pity he doesn't have a job.

September 27

Got back the latest cut of the video. Don't ask.

September 30

Very discouraged. Scott in the hospital again.

Raising My Titanic

October 8

Scott home again.

October 13

Molly has made a new friend at school. A little boy named Jake. When I asked Molly why she had chosen Jake as her special friend, she said, "I feel sorry for him. He smells bad and no one else wants to play with him." I feel very proud of Molly for this nobility of character, and can only hope that it will wear off by the time she's ready to choose a boyfriend.

October 20

Big news. Edward and I have done the deed.

Molly was with Mitch last night, and Edward came over. We had dinner, then sat on my bed and watched *Big Wednesday,* a movie about the early days of surfing.

Then suddenly he leaned over and kissed me. It didn't even take any fishnet stockings or incense.

Edward as a lover is like he is as a man—gentle and shy and spiritual. Perhaps even a little too spiritual? He gets so wrapped up in the mysticism of the event that he tends to forget the physical side. I suppose that's a sign of his being highly evolved.

As for me, I'm confused. Feel relief and anxiety at the same time. One part of my mind is saying, "Congratulations. You're finally involved with a decent guy—don't worry about the future; just enjoy the present."

And the other part is screaming, "When the hell is this man going to get a job?"

October 21

A prayer answered! Edward just called, saying he has an interview for a sales position later this afternoon. I'm excited. This could be the beginning of something substantial.

October 22

Well, Edward's interview didn't work out. But it wasn't really his fault. He had the job all sewn up. Then at the last second, he made one little joke about the owner's Masarati. The guy had no sense of humor and ended up giving the job to someone else.

Raising My Titanic

October 24

Got another cut of the video. Great progress. Only twenty-six glitches left.

October 25

I just heard the news. Married less than four months, and Amy Matthews and her husband are separating. Just goes to show you. All that jealousy I felt at her happiness—I feel so ashamed.

Incidentally, speaking of relationships, Molly has started asking a lot of questions about Edward. She even says she wants to meet him. I told her I'd arrange something soon. I'm a little nervous but tell myself that, this time, I have no reason to be. Edward's so gentle and childlike—he's sure to win her over.

October 26

Spent the day getting Molly's Halloween costume all ready. This year she wants to go as Marilyn Monroe. Sequined bathing-suit top, long ballet skirt bottom, and—as we all know—I have a sexy blonde wig to provide. She looks adorable.

October 30

Molly has changed her mind. She and her friend Jake have decided to go trick-or-treating together, and I have less than twenty-four hours to come up with costumes for them.

Anyway, I sat on the sofa and wondered what on Earth I was going to do—and then I thought of Helen Butler.

When I was eight years old, Helen Butler was my best friend in the whole world. She was a skinny little girl with Huck Finn freckles and white eyelashes. Her temper was uncertain, and she watched wrestling—but I loved her anyway.

That Halloween, our third-grade class was having a contest for best costume. Mama, who sewed like a dream, rigged Helen and me out as a miniature Antony and Cleopatra, and we won first prize.

Looking back, I truly think that winning that blue ribbon was one of the most important moments of my childhood. Up to that point, I had never won anything. I had just been a kid, happy to be like the other kids. But that October day, when I walked up to the stage to accept that first-prize award, something happened inside me. I got hooked. Hooked on competing, hooked on winning, hooked on blue ribbons.

Raising My Titanic

Halloween

What a night. What a night.

As soon as it was dusk, I left work and raced home. A madly excited Molly and Jake were waiting for me to help them into their costumes. After many last-minute alterations, and much criticism from Molly (unlike my mother, I do not sew like a dream), the kids were finally ready, and we drove down to the Sherman Oaks Galleria to trick-or-treat. The place was filled—packed, crushed—with sugar-rushed vampires, witches, hula girls. All the stores were open, and giving out candy. Molly and Jake trick-or-treated for an hour, and then an announcement was made. It was time for the big costume contest.

I hadn't even known there was going to be a big costume contest—but the instant I heard the words, boom. Something snapped. Before my own eyes, I turned back into that third-grader whose whole life was winning blue ribbons.

I went into overdrive. I spent ten minutes relentlessly coaching the kids—how they should walk, how Jake should use his spear, how Molly should hold her asp.

The contest began. About a million children crossed that stage. Dreadfully cutesy little wretches, conceited little prigs, pathetic little losers—I hated them all. And I especially hated the kids in the really good costumes—the boy who was dressed as a carton of toxic waste, the beautiful little girl who went as a geisha dancer.

Finally, it was Molly and Jake's turn. They walked slowly out in front of the audience. Molly looked beautiful, like a precious porcelain figurine. Seeing her up there on that vast stage, it was all I could do to control myself from screaming with pride, "That firework is *mine*!"

Half an hour later, when all the costumes had been seen, the judges conferred, then finally stepped onstage.

Four ribbons were being given out. Fourth Place was announced: the geisha girl. Third Place was announced: a boy dressed as a Southern Belle. Second Place was announced: a girl dressed as a Rubic's Cube. And then the room hushed.

"And the First Place winner is—entry number 73!"

Molly and Jake were Number 73.

I watched, dumb with tears, as my little girl and her friend walked up onstage to claim their blue ribbon. Jake was blushing, Molly was silent and poised.

My whole life of superachievement flashed before my eyes: the joy of those special moments of victory, the undeniable fact that they made everything worthwhile. And I knew that Molly had now officially started on the track, too.

For better or worse, she's going to be another me. Yes, the prison doors may close around her—but at least she'll be a winner in prison.

Sniffling back tears, I rushed forward and nearly knocked her over with the force of my hug.

Raising My Titanic

And then I made an interesting discovery, that maybe Molly isn't another me after all.

As I came up to her, she was handing Jake the blue ribbon.

"Here," she said. "You can have it if you want."

"But don't you want it?" Jake asked, awed.

"No," Molly said. "Blue doesn't match my room."

November 4

Video finally winding down. I can't believe it. Only three glitches left to go.

November 6

Scott feeling well enough to come to brunch with Molly and me yesterday. She hadn't seen him in a while, and though I'd told her he'd been sick, she kept asking me in a whisper why he was so thin, and why he was walking with a cane. Don't know what to say. Don't know how to prepare her.

November 7

Molly and Edward are finally going to meet. Am excited.

November 8

Molly and Edward have finally met. Am depressed.

He came over at two, bringing a bouquet of flowers for her; but Molly took an instant dislike to him. She told him he showed too much of his gums when he smiled, and that she didn't believe for one minute that he could surf.

We went to a movie, which none of us liked, then to an early dinner. When we got home, Edward didn't say much about Molly—except to point out how differently the children he's used to (sons and daughters of vegetarian meditators) behave. I almost said something like "Wait till you've tried being a parent before you start judging," but then I decided that he's probably right. I'm sure, from Edward's perspective, Molly and I both have a lot of growing to do.

Came into her room after he left, intending to have a talk with her that would scar her for life. But she looked so withdrawn and sad that I didn't have the heart. Instead, I held up the one finger, the *You are my number one* sign. We cuddled a bit,

Raising My Titanic

then she went to sleep. But I can't get her resigned, too-old-for-her-years look out of my mind. Maybe I'm scarring her for life without even trying.

November 9

Good news! Edward has gotten a telemarketing job, and he starts tomorrow! This could change everything. Give him some steady work, and who knows what might happen?

November 11

The new job didn't work out. Everyone at the office was smoking, and Edward's allergies started acting up. I suggested he take some Teldrin, but he said he didn't want to pollute his body. So he quit the job instead. He's interviewing at another firm next week though—one run by nonsmoking Buddhists.

November 13

The video is done done *done*!

There is still one mistake in it, but to me it looks like *Gone with the Wind.*

I showed it to Edward last night. He said that while he appreciated all the work that had doubtless gone into it, frankly, he wasn't impressed, said he couldn't really relate to something so commercial. Considered dumping the bowl of pretzels on his head, but luckily, a little hard-won maturity stepped in. The thing to remember is that Edward's standards are very high. After all, he lives in the world of Kurosawa and Tarkovsky. Of course he's not going to think much of *The Strawberry Parfait.*

Hoped for a romantic evening to make up for the disappointment, but he said he had exhausted himself doing yoga, and went home early.

November 15

Edward started his new job at the Buddhist place today. But he ate a piece of cheese at lunch, and that ruined everything. He's very sensitive to dairy products, and it threw off his whole system. He fell asleep during work, the boss happened to pass by, and he got fired.

But he's going on a meditation retreat over Thanksgiving. That should get his energy back up.

Raising My Titanic

November 22

Happy Thanksgiving. Had a nice time. Scott and Cheryl came over for dinner, and we all laughed like maniacs. Then afterward, we all sat around listening to Simon and Garfunkel songs and playing Candyland with Molly. She managed to win every game. Luck—or is she playing a system?

In the middle of the evening I heard a horn honking irascibly below my window. It turned out to be Peter. Scowling furiously, he came up to the apartment and handed over a stunning pumpkin pie. He stayed long enough to have a piece and to be beaten by the Queen of Candyland. He is not a good loser.

Later

Am sitting over one lorn last sliver of pie. The dishes are all done, the place looks sweet and shining. Molly is in bed, clutching her Goofy doll and her winning Candyland game token.

Happy Thanksgiving.

THINGS TO BE THANKFUL FOR

1. My precious little girl, with all her winds and weathers.

2. Scott and Cheryl and Peter.

3. Health and almost enough money.

4. The little things that make life worthwhile: *I Love Lucy* reruns, the love scene in *Emma,* Bavarian mints, Merchant-Ivory films, the Persian cat at the pet store, honey-creme bath oil, Brahms's Second Symphony, Sam and Libby shoes, memories of my parents, Buddy's letters.

4. And I'm so grateful for all that I've learned this year.

But I must admit it; I'm feeling a little annoyed with Edward. He hasn't called once all weekend. Tell myself that maybe there aren't any phones in the meditation center. Do not really believe this for a second.

November 23

Feeling of slight annoyance is turning into feeling of major fury. Edward is back from the retreat and he came over last night. He said that there had been phones, but that he had needed his time alone.

I reasonably suggested that since he had so successfully achieved his time alone, he might now be interested in spending some time alone with *me*. Put on my purple teddy, to emphasize the point. But Edward said he didn't want to lower the new

Raising My Titanic

consciousness he had gained during the retreat, and he left early. Threw purple teddy in the trash compactor.

November 26

Can't believe it. Came into work this morning, and was called into Peter's office. He looked even grimmer than usual. And then he tersely informed me that he is throwing a party at Trader Vic's for me tomorrow night, in honor of my having finished the video. I almost burst into tears, but of course did no such thing. I only glared back at Peter, in the same way he was glaring at me, and told him grimly that, if no better offer came up, I would try to be there.

November 27

Called up Edward and invited him to the party. He didn't sound too enthusiastic about going, said the energy at parties tends to throw him off balance; but he finally agreed to take me. What a hero.

6:00 P.M.

Just got a call from Edward. He can't take me to the party. He was on his way over to pick me up, when he saw a poor old man in a wheelchair, trying to cross Westwood Boulevard. Edward stopped—one thing led to another—and it ended up with his promising the old man that he would wheel him all the way down to Santa Monica.

He says he's sure I'll understand, that helping out a human being in need is a lot more important than a social event.

No comment.

November 28

Had a fabulous time at the party. Ended up taking Molly as my date. She was thrilled to go. Without any prompting from me, she got all dressed up in her little tuxedo.

The whole office turned up, and even some of our celebrity readers. There was champagne, a cake saying "Congratulations," and Peter gave a speech, saying how shocked he was at what a good job I had done on the video.

After the speech, I went into the ladies' room to have a cry. When I came back, there was Molly, standing up on Peter's chair, and belting out the song "You Gotta Have a Gimmick" to the entire admiring restaurant.

Can only be grateful Edward wasn't there to hear her.

Raising My Titanic

November 29

A heat spell of astonishing proportions. It's in the high eighties. Everyone is going around dressed in shorts and tank tops. Only in California.

One fun thing. Edward is taking Molly and me to the beach tomorrow. I'm finally going to see him surf. I'm excited about it. In some strange way I feel that seeing him doing what he's best at will be a great restorative to our relationship. It will remind me of why I was attracted to him in the first place.

November 30

Back from the beach. It was quite a day. Molly and I have seen Edward surf. Or rather, we have seen Edward try to surf. He made eleven attempts, but somehow he just couldn't seem to get up on the board.

We watched him for over an hour.

It was painful. It was really painful.

"I told you," Molly kept saying with satisfaction. "I told you he couldn't surf."

When Edward came back to shore, he was full of explanations.

His knee hurt, the waves were going in all the wrong directions, the ocean had been too crowded....

And all of a sudden, something exploded inside me.

The scales have not only dropped from my eyes, they have crashed onto the ground, making a crater the size of Kansas City. How could I have been such a patsy? All those sad stories from Edward's past, all those failed interviews, all those failed jobs, all those failed relationships. No, it didn't all happen because Edward was unlucky. Or because his parents were so awful. Or because he's too pure for this Earth. It happened, when you get right down to it, because Edward simply can't ride the wave.

He drove me home in silence. Something Scott once told me kept running through my head. "There are two kinds of people: those who have what they want, and those who have excuses for not having what they want."

When we got back to my apartment, I told Edward as gently as I could that I didn't want to see him anymore. He snapped back that that was just fine with him. That as he had come to know me better he had come to realize that I wasn't the kind of evolved woman he wanted to be with anyway.

Feel a little taken aback, but I look at it this way—I may be a spiritual lowlife, but at least I got the video done.

Raising My Titanic

December 1

Molly came home from Mitch's tonight, with the bombshell to end all bombshells. Just call me Dresden. Just call me Hiroshima.

Mitch and Veronica are going to have a baby.

You may not be surprised to learn that this news has thrown me into depths of self-pity and self-questioning that make Hamlet look like a character from *Sesame Street*.

SEVERAL VERY GOOD REASONS
WHY MITCH AND VERONICA SHOULD
NOT HAVE A BABY

1. There are too many babies already in the world. Where's Mitch's sense of social responsibility?

2. I don't have a baby.

I cannot believe I just wrote that sentence. But I'm staring at this computer screen, and there it is. My God. Up until this minute, I never even thought I wanted another baby. But now I realize what an abject failure I truly am. Career, friends, my nice apartment, even Molly—they're all dust to me now. Why can't I have another baby?

MARY SHELDON

REASONS WHY IT'S STUPID
TO WANT A BABY

1. I'm not married. I don't even have a boyfriend. I don't even have a date.

2. I already have the best baby in the world.

3. I have spent the last five years waiting for her to grow and not be a baby anymore, so I could have a semblance of a life again. Do I really want to go back to square one?

A baby. A shrieking, two o'clock in the morning, diaper-wetting, refusing-to-eat, falling-out-of-its-crib-and-needing-stitches baby.

Yes, yes, yes!

I think I'd better go back to the therapist.

Later

I made up my mind to rise above this insane envy. I decided that, instead of being resentful of Mitch and Veronica's baby, I would welcome it as if it were going to be my own. So I consciously embraced the thought of this special new life.

During my lunch hour, I went into the baby boutique that's just opened up on Santa Monica Boulevard. Tenderly, I went through racks of tiny outfits and chose a darling white knitted jumper. I had it gift wrapped and wrote a card. First I wrote one

Raising My Titanic

that said, "Love from Betty and Molly," then tore it up and wrote a second that was just from Molly. Mitch and Veronica will like that one a lot better.

Then, as I was leaving the store, I saw the cutest item I have ever laid eyes on. It was a tiny James Dean–like leather jacket with a fur collar—the perfect gift for a newborn baby boy who lives in Alaska. I do not know any newborn baby boys who live in Alaska. But I had to buy the jacket. I needed it. I absolutely needed it.

The jacket ended up costing more than my last year's winter coat. The lady behind the counter asked me if I wanted it gift wrapped. I didn't want her to get suspicious, so I said, "Of course." She took so long wrapping it that I was late back to work and spent the afternoon being punished by Peter's outraged glares.

Later

Am still trying to rationalize the jacket. Find I cannot.

But picture this interesting scene. Fifty years from now, when I'm dead (that is, if Cancer of the Month doesn't get me first) and the weeping relatives clean out my closet, they'll come upon this dusty little gift-wrapped box. They'll open it up and find the tiny jacket; and everyone will wonder and wonder.

Perhaps it will even inspire a sequel to *Citizen Kane*.

December 4

Oh, my God. It was just a joke. I swear, I meant it as a joke.

This can't be happening. I don't want Edward's baby. I don't want a baby who can't do a damn thing in life, not even surf.

What should I do? We haven't even spoken since we broke up. Should I tell him? Not tell him? Should I have the baby? Not have the baby?

If I have the baby, I'll be ostracized. I'll have to move to another state. Or country. And Mitch will get custody of Molly, because I'm a bad moral influence. But could I get rid of the baby? I don't believe I could. How ironic. I've always been so adamantly pro-choice—until the choice is mine.

Well, nothing to panic about yet. I'm only three days late, after all. Perhaps I just counted wrong. Perhaps it's a cold, or stress. I'll wait another week or so, and if nothing's happened by then I'll take one of those home pregnancy tests.

Later

Couldn't wait out the week. Went out at lunchtime and bought the test. Had the store double-wrap it in two brown bags and a couple of plastic ones. And then I went furtively into the office bathroom and locked the door.

Raising My Titanic

Read the directions four times. You mix a drop of urine with this powder, and pour the whole thing into a little well. If the dot in the middle of the well turns pink, you're pregnant. The only problem is, the dot is already pink to begin with. It's a question of how much pinker does it get?

The test thoughtfully provides a little chart. If it's this shade of pink, you're okay. If it's this shade of pink, you're doomed.

I took the test. I had to wait sixty seconds for the results; and I got so faint from tension that I was reduced to having to lie full-length down on the floor of the restroom.

Finally, with shaking hands, I picked up the little vial. The dot was pink. Yes but was it pink-pink, or merely pink? I couldn't tell. I simply couldn't tell. I squinted. I held it under the fluorescent light. I sneaked it into the hall and looked at it from there. But the well was about half an inch deep, and hard to look at without shadows interfering. I even risked taking it to the office and looking at it by a window. But I still couldn't tell. Finally I took the test book and snipped off samples of the two shades of pink. Like some insane interior decorator checking swatches, I held them against the dot in the well. Was it the pink of relief or the pink of doom? I still couldn't tell.

Finally, with five minutes of my lunch hour to go, I raced back to the drugstore and bought a different brand of pregnancy test. The fellow behind the desk looked at me in a way I do not wish to remember.

This time I selected the mathematical motif: a plus sign appears if you're pregnant, a minus sign if you're not. Back to the ladies' room. Back to coaxing my poor overworked kidneys to give their all. Took the test. Back to lying on the bathroom floor. Waited sixty seconds. And then, there it was—a big beautiful minus sign.

So I'm not pregnant. I'm not going to be ostracized, not going to lose Molly, not going to have to deal with Edward, the ne'er-do-well father of a nonsurfing baby.

And now, of course, I'm feeling regret.

December 6

Had a great night. Peter, in a fit of pre-Christmas generosity, gave me two tickets to a huge Women in Film gala. I invited Scott. He wasn't sure until the last minute if he'd be up to going, but he made it and off we went to the Beverly Center. After the film, we were supposed to assemble downstairs later to hear all the speeches. But Scott started to get tired, so we decided to sneak out. We looked down on all the poor suckers below, getting ready to be bored by speechifying, and we plotted our escape. We couldn't take the escalators—too visible. So we decided to take the elevator instead.

We got in, pushed the button, and realized—too late. The elevator was glass and our escape could be seen and discussed and disapproved of by every guest in the Beverly Center.

Raising My Titanic

And then, halfway between floors, the elevator stopped dead. My two worst nightmares were cunningly intermingled, being trapped in a motionless elevator, and making a fool of myself in front of five hundred people. Half an hour later, we were released by a security guard. I think I shall stop shopping in the Beverly Center.

Scott and I finished up the evening by getting drunk. We laughed and we laughed and we laughed. I don't think I've ever had such a good time in my life.

December 9

Scott is dead. The landlady found him in his apartment this morning. It happened in his sleep. Very quick. No pain.

I keep hanging onto that. That and how much we loved each other. And all our laughter the other night.

But I don't really believe it. Not for a minute. How can Scott not be there anymore?

How can Molly grow up in a world without Scott? How can I?

December 11

Peter came into my office this morning and told me that I have been nominated for a Spoken Word Grammy, for the Elliot Frobisher tape, the one that was phoned in over my answering machine, essay by essay. This is it. This is the thing I thought I had been looking forward to ever since I entered this business.

I can't tell you how little it means to me.

December 13

Went to Scott's memorial service today. It was very beautiful. His family flew in from the East and I finally got to meet them. There was a big blown-up picture of Scott on the dais. It must have been taken when he was about eighteen—he had a guitar, and long hair, and he was laughing. A lot of people got up and talked about him. It made me feel so high listening to those great Scott stories and seeing that dear laughing face.

I kept thinking with such joy, wow, wow, what a great person. What a great person this is. And then remembering that it is all over.

There is no more Scott. If I call his number, he will not answer. I'll never hear his voice again. Never. There will be no more lunches at tacky little Mexican restaurants. No more good

Raising My Titanic

times. No more wise words. He and Molly and I will never make a perfect shadow family again. Ever. Whatever happens to me in my life from now on, good or bad, Scott will not be a part of it.

I feel very weary of life. There's no sense in anything.

December 15

I grow more and more depressed. Spent the morning reading over this diary. Boy, is my life pathetic.

All year long, I've done nothing but jump from one frantic work project to another, from one bout of insecurity with Molly to another, from one obviously doomed relationship to another. Not one entry in this diary shows any modicum of growth or maturity.

And the worst part is, I read somewhere recently that if you keep on in the direction you're headed, sooner or later, you're bound to end up there. This does not bode well at all.

I can see into the future, ten years from today, as if it were spread out on a map. Molly will be in the throes of rampant teenagedom. Peter will have grown into mature curmudgeonliness. I will be skinny and frazzled (or fat and frazzled), trying desperately to maintain my job, keep everyone happy, and find a soul mate among the parade of over-the-hill gigolos that Cheryl will supply.

And Mitch, of course, will by this time have become president of the United States.

December 18

I think I may have a plan. I think I'm going to follow Aunt Becky's advice and move up to Seattle.

It'll be a pure, healthy life, a fresh start. I'll like the coffee, Molly will like the camping. And maybe I will, too, when I get some more appropriate pajamas. Or, better yet, maybe we'll move somewhere down South, where life is slower, and people are warm. No more pressure. No more Hollywood phonies. No more men who are maniacs. Maybe we'll move to Colonial Williamsburg. Maybe I'll be one of the docents, and wear a mob cap. And never be heard of in this century again.

December 19

I threw out the suggestion to Molly tonight. That in a few months, we might be moving.

I thought she'd be so excited. But the first words out of her mouth were "What about Daddy? When will I be seeing Daddy?" And she kept saying it, over and over and over. I explained that

Raising My Titanic

of course we'd work all that out—that she'd be with Mitch on vacations, etc. But inside I was dying.

It killed me that in the moment it really counted, Mitch is the one she loves, not me. It killed me that Molly's first knee-jerk reaction was not about the two of us, not about the move. It was Daddy—what about Daddy.

I totally lost control. I yelled at her. I screamed at her. I told her how much it hurt me that she loved Mitch so much more than she loved me. And finally I gave in. I did something I never thought I would do. I told her that if she wanted, she didn't have to make the move with me. She could stay in Los Angeles with Mitch and Veronica.

She left the room.

She came back a few minutes later. I expected to see her little packed suitcase. But there was none.

She looked at me very seriously, and said in a stern grown-up voice, "Mama, we need to talk. I think there's something you should know."

And she held up one shy little finger.

Number One. I was her Number One.

I almost drowned her with my sobs.

December 20

Frantic Christmas shopping. Incredible to think that this will be our last Christmas in Los Angeles.

List of Things I'm Going to Miss

1. Speeding down Loma Vista on sparkling winter nights.

2. The moments when the smog clears and you get the feeling of what it must have been like in the twenties, when the air smelled of orange blossom.

3. Peter telling me I'm fired.

4. Cheryl's crazed schemes.

5. All my little hangouts and discoveries, the coffee shop where I get the best cappuccino in the world, the tiny garden off Sunset, the witch's house on Carmelita. (Where will I get Sam and Libby shoes in Seattle? Gently used designer clothes in Dallas? Find a really good psychic in Williamsburg? Well, I'll manage.)

6. The view from my window.

7. The fact that Scott lived here, and is buried here.

Raising My Titanic

The fact that my parents lived here and are buried here.

8. The fact that all my memories—and all of Molly's memories—are of here. Mama bought me my first swimsuit at Saks department store on Wilshire. I bought Molly her first swimsuit at Neiman Marcus department store on Wilshire. I threw my first temper tantrum at the park on Santa Monica. Molly threw her first temper tantrum on Pico Boulevard. I had my third birthday party at Kiddieland. She had her third birthday party at the zoo. It was from Santa Monica Beach that I first saw the ocean. It was from Venice Beach that she first saw the ocean. Here that I first went to Disneyland. Here that she first went to Disneyland.

Our whole lives have been Los Angeles lives.

I can't believe that we're leaving this city. I can't believe it, but we're doing it anyway.

December 22

Something very amazing has happened.

I was getting dressed to go out last night—the office is holding

MARY SHELDON

its annual party—and I wasn't any too happy to hear the phone ring. I told Molly to answer it and to tell whoever it was that I would call back tomorrow. Well, she picked up the phone and stayed on it for ten minutes. I couldn't hear what she was saying, but since she wasn't hanging up, I figured the call was for her, probably her friend Jake.

When I came out of the bedroom, she was still on the phone. I said that I had to go and wanted to say goodbye to her; could she call her friend back in a few minutes? She said the phone call wasn't for her—that it was for me.

Very puzzled, I picked up the receiver. It was Buddy Villiers.

I couldn't believe it. I couldn't believe it. I started to cry. It was like hearing a voice from the dead. I asked him where he was calling from. He said from Los Angeles. I asked if he and his wife were visiting; he said no. He said that he and his wife had been divorced for the past two years—that he had simply gotten homesick and had decided to move back to Los Angeles. He's here for good.

He said he'd love to see me. I didn't know what to say. I said sure. I invited him over here tomorrow. He said he'd come by after I finish work.

I feel overwhelmed, incoherent. It's like I have Scott back, or my parents. No, that's not it. It's more like I have my whole childhood back. Myself back.

I can't believe it. Buddy Villiers.

December 23

It's noon. I'll be seeing Buddy in six hours. Am starting to feel slightly sick about the whole thing.

I've thought it over, and I've decided to cancel. This reunion is a very bad idea.

REASONS I'M CANCELING

1. I am thirty-one. I am old and ugly. Buddy hasn't seen me in well over a decade. It's going to be a terrible shock.

2. My memories of that relationship are so wonderful. They've always been such a comfort. No subsequent meeting can possibly live up to them. What if we just sit and chitchat like strangers?

3. Or what if we simply don't like each other any more? No. That's not what I'm worried about. I know I'll still like Buddy. What I'm worried about is that he will no longer like me.

   Buddy once loved me so much. Buddy once thought I was the most wonderful person in the world. And he had this special way of looking at me. It has always meant so much to me, knowing that there was always one person in my life who looked at me like that.

What if we see each other tonight, and that look is no longer there? What do I mean, *what if*? Of course it's not going to be there. Thirteen years have passed. I'm old and ugly. And Buddy's no longer a kid. By this time, he's seen far better things than me.

4. And then, of course, there's Molly. Buddy's always been such a precious memory to me. I can't bear to see him spurned by Molly, the man-hater.

Anyway, I'm canceling the date. It's sad but very clear. My relationship with Buddy belongs to the past, and that's where it's going to stay.

Called Buddy at the number he gave me. Left a message on the machine, saying I had had to go out of town, and that I would call back when I return. But I won't call back.

I feel terrible about it. But I know I'm doing the right thing.

Later

I can't believe it.

I came home from work tonight, grouchy and a total mess. As I walked in the door, I could hear Molly talking in the living room. The baby-sitter came up to me at the door.

Raising My Titanic

"Your friend's here," she said.

My friend was here? *Buddy?*

I just about burst into tears. What could have happened? Hadn't he gotten my message? If he had come when we had scheduled, that meant that he had been here—unprotected—with Molly for the last half hour. As I turned, I caught sight of the vision I presented in the mirror, and had fresh reason for tears. I looked hideous. I had to get to the bathroom. I must somehow put on makeup, brush my hair.

But Molly heard me.

"Mama! Mama!" she cried. "We're in here!"

I froze. But I didn't have a choice.

I walked into the living room.

Buddy was there on the sofa. And I saw three things all in the same split second.

The first was that Molly was sitting on his lap and clinging to his neck.

The second was that he hadn't changed one single bit since high school.

And the third was the way he was looking at me. That hadn't changed since high school either.

We just stared at each other. I didn't trust myself to say a word.

"Well, I'm starved," Molly complained. "I want Buddy to take us to McDonald's and then to a movie."

February 10

Buddy and I took Molly to the park today. Buddy held one side of the bicycle, I held the other, and Molly pedaled like a little demon. The bicycle got faster and lighter and straighter—and then, at the same moment, we let go.

And Molly was bicycling at last.

We cheered and we cheered and we cheered.